JANE AUSTEN'S
SENSE AND SENSIBILITY

RETOLD BY JOANNA NADIN
ILLUSTRATED BY ÉGLANTINE CEULEMANS

HODDER

HODDER CHILDREN'S BOOKS

First published in Great Britain in 2020 by Hodder & Stoughton

1 3 5 7 9 10 8 6 4 2

Text copyright © Joanna Nadin, 2020
Illustrations copyright © Églantine Ceulemans, 2020

The moral right of the author has been asserted.

A CIP catalogue record for this book
is available from the British Library.

ISBN 978 1 444 95067 0

Typeset in Bembo by Hewer Text UK Ltd, Edinburgh
Printed and bound in Great Britain by Clays Ltd, Elcograf S.p.A

The paper and board used in this book
are made from wood from responsible sources.

Hodder Children's Books
An imprint of
Hachette Children's Group
Part of Hodder & Stoughton
Carmelite House
50 Victoria Embankment
London, EC4Y 0DZ

An Hachette UK Company
www.hachette.co.uk

www.hachettechildrens.co.uk

Sense and Sensibility, by Jane Austen, was first published in 1811.

This was the Regency era — a time when English society was sharply divided by wealth and women were expected to marry young.

The heroines of this story, Elinor and Marianne, might have some things in common with modern readers, but they lived in a very different world.

You can find out more about Jane Austen and what England was like in 1811 at the back of this book!

MAIN CHARACTERS

MR HENRY DASHWOOD
Father of one son and three daughters. He dies before the start of the story.

MRS DASHWOOD
Henry's second wife and loving mother of three daughters.

MISS MARIANNE DASHWOOD
The middle Dashwood sister. Marianne is a romantic and often very dramatic.

MISS ELINOR DASHWOOD
Wise and affectionate, Elinor is the eldest Dashwood sister.

MISS MARGARET DASHWOOD
The youngest Dashwood sister. Margaret is good-humoured but can be naive at times.

MR JOHN DASHWOOD
The Dashwood sisters' half-brother. He is easily influenced by his wife. Lives at Norland Estate after his father's death.

MRS FANNY DASHWOOD
John's husband. Fanny is selfish, greedy and manipulative.

HENRY DASHWOOD
The young son of John and Fanny.

COLONEL BRANDON
The Colonel is a serious yet compassionate man. He is older than the Dashwood sisters.

MR JOHN WILLOUGHBY
An attractive yet deceitful man, hiding many secrets.

MRS FERRARS
The mother of Fanny, Edward and Robert. She is an arrogant, unfriendly woman.

MR EDWARD FERRARS
Fanny's brother. Edward is kind-hearted and sensible unlike the rest of his family.

MR ROBERT FERRARS
Fanny's brother. Robert is thought of by many as a fool and a show-off.

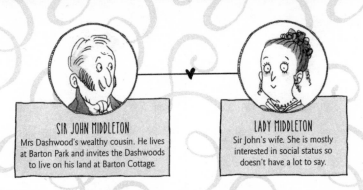

SIR JOHN MIDDLETON
Mrs Dashwood's wealthy cousin. He lives at Barton Park and invites the Dashwoods to live on his land at Barton Cottage.

LADY MIDDLETON
Sir John's wife. She is mostly interested in social status so doesn't have a lot to say.

MRS JENNINGS
Lady Middleton's cousin. Mrs Jennings is a lively woman who loves to gossip and matchmake.

MRS CHARLOTTE PALMER
Mrs Jennings' youngest daughter. Charlotte is an enthusiastic, talkative woman.

MR THOMAS PALMER
The unemotional, sour husband of Charlotte.

MISS NANCY STEELE
A distant cousin of Mrs Jennings. Nancy is foolish and flippant with her comments.

MISS LUCY STEELE
A distant cousin of Mrs Jennings. Lucy appears quiet and reserved but has a sly side.

CHAPTER ONE

In life, Mr Henry Dashwood adored all his children equally.

There was John, his first-born, whose heart was, at least originally, in the right place, but who was too easily led by his wife, Fanny Dashwood. Her selfish and greedy ways soon rubbed off on him.

Then there was his eldest daughter, sensible Elinor, whose calm demeanour and wisdom balanced out her slightly flighty mother, Mrs Dashwood (Henry's second wife and John's stepmother). Next was the middle sister, Marianne, whose romantic sensibilities led her to either weeping or shrieking with delight on an almost daily basis.

Last of all came Margaret, who, at thirteen, was still of an age where she found the rules of society somewhat odd. Not least the one that dictated that, despite her father's equal affection, when he died he had to leave his entire estate – their beloved home of Norland – to John, on account of him being male and therefore somehow more deserving.

'Not his "entire" estate,' pointed out Elinor. 'We have a thousand pounds each.'

'Who's going to marry us on that?' protested

Marianne. 'We're practically paupers!'

Their mother sighed in agreement.

'Not quite paupers,' said Elinor. 'And anyway, I thought "true love" didn't care about income or status?'

'I suppose,' begrudged Marianne, recalling her own words from a month before. 'But I still don't think it's fair that John gets the house.'

'Not when he already has one in London,' said Margaret, still weighing up the injustice of it all.

'Well, perhaps he won't want it,' suggested Elinor, ever the peacekeeper. 'Perhaps we shall be able to stay as long as we want. That would be fair, I think.'

Perhaps John hadn't sought Norland for himself, but the decision, alas, wasn't up to him alone, and 'fairness' was not in his wife's vocabulary, as Mrs Dashwood and her daughters were about to find out.

CHAPTER TWO

No sooner had Fanny received news that John had inherited the Norland estate, the family's bags were packed and she, her husband and their son, the overly doted-on Henry, set out for Norland, which Fanny was already referring to as their 'country residence'.

'Of course, there will need to be alterations,' she declared, as the carriage clattered its way from London to Sussex. 'Improvements too; it's so very outdated, after all. And the dust! What the servants do all day I am quite at a loss to know.'

'Yes, dear,' agreed John, though he wasn't at all clear what he was agreeing to, lost as he was in his

own thoughts of inheritance. 'Perhaps I should give them another thousand apiece,' he mused out loud. 'That would be generous, wouldn't it? I think it would look good.'

'A thousand pounds each?' Fanny's face paled. 'That's three thousand less a year for precious Henry! Rob your own boy, would you?'

John shrank. 'Well, now that you put it like

that.' He thought again. 'Five hundred each? Papa did ask me to make sure they were all right once he was no longer around.'

'He'd probably lost his senses when he said that. He was ill, after all. And what will they want with the money when they move to a modest house? There'll be no need for horses, for servants – and when they marry, whose hands will our money be in?'

'Yes, quite right,' admitted John.

'Good.'

As ever, Fanny got the last word, as, within moments, the carriage turned up the sweeping drive to Norland and all members of the party fell silent at the sight of the house that was now theirs by law, however unfair that might seem to some.

★ ★ ★

While John, Fanny and Henry were delighted at their arrival, the Dashwoods were quite put out, not least by the fact that Fanny hadn't even given them notice.

'Notice?' she repeated, handing her umbrella and gloves to a servant, others bustling behind them, carrying their many bags. 'To our own residence? How absurd.'

The truth, if it hadn't hit them already, was now as clear as a crystal champagne glass: the Dashwoods were rendered visitors in their own home. Even Mrs Dashwood, who saw the good in everyone and was usually so tolerant of fools (sometimes to a worrying degree), seethed at this sudden injustice. 'The nerve of her,' she snapped. 'Complaining about the dust.'

'I heard her say she's going to get rid of the library on account of it,' cried Marianne. 'Papa's books!' And she began to sob.

'Heathen,' agreed Margaret, passing Marianne a handkerchief.

Only Elinor was able to keep her fury in check. 'There's no point in getting cross,' she said calmly. 'We have to plan, and that means finding a new house.'

At that, both Mrs Dashwood and Marianne cried out, but the truth was upon them, and once she had dried her eyes, Mrs Dashwood did begin to plan, discussing over the coming days details of houses she thought she might be able to tolerate.

Once again, Elinor had to play wise parent. 'Mama, these are all fine houses, but they are beyond our means. We are . . . reduced now and must cut our cloth accordingly.'

'You'd have us live in a hovel,' protested Marianne.

'I shouldn't mind,' said Margaret. 'I'd rather a hovel than live with Fanny any longer, and besides, think of the adventure!'

'I don't want an adventure,' wailed Marianne. 'I want my piano! And my horse!'

'Not a hovel,' corrected Elinor. 'A cottage.'

'You can't keep a horse at a cottage,' pointed out Marianne.

'No,' agreed Elinor. 'But we can live comfortably and, more importantly, together.'

In this, at least, they were in agreement.

CHAPTER THREE

Elinor was still sifting through sketches of prospective cottages, hoping that her mother wouldn't refuse all of them, when Fanny exercised her newfound status as Lady of the House by announcing that her brother was coming to stay.

'Which one?' asked Elinor, having knowledge of two men as unalike, it was widely reported, as a pea and a peppercorn.

'Edward,' said Fanny. 'Not that it matters.'

But matter it did, and a great deal. For Edward Ferrars was a far different prospect from Robert (a fool and a show-off if ever there was one), and from his sister Fanny too. Where Fanny, taking after her mother, enjoyed money and craved even more of it, Edward did not care for either career or fortune. All he'd ever wanted was to become a vicar in a quiet country village. An idea that antagonised his family enormously.

The Dashwoods, however, warmed to him the moment he arrived.

'Such a kind man,' declared Mrs Dashwood.

'And rich,' said Margaret. 'Though he doesn't boast about it at all.'

'The church, though?' said Marianne, baffled by the prospect.

'His mother wants him to go into parliament,' said Elinor, who had been discussing the sad matter with him only that morning. 'But he cannot bear the idea.'

'Well, he's too old for the army,' said Mrs Dashwood.

'And "not smart enough" for the navy,' said Elinor. 'That was his joke. Though he is wrong, of course.'

Marianne pulled a face. 'He's hardly handsome though. And so . . . awkward. When he reads aloud it's as dull as the worst kind of sermon.'

'He's just shy,' retorted Elinor, surprised at her own defensiveness, and wondering what to make of it, as surely her mother was as well.

Her dear mother, driven, as were so many of her gender, by the prospect of a good match, had done exactly that and found to her delight that Elinor was obviously falling in love. She hoped that Edward would too, given enough time. And so, she dallied further over choosing a cottage, endeavouring to keep Elinor in Edward's company as long as she could, ignoring the bickering of her daughters, who could still not agree over either his virtues, or Elinor's affection.

'His taste is so unrefined,' complained Marianne. 'He has no ear for music and though he claims to like your sketches, it's only because they're *yours*, not because he understands why they're good.'

'Well, doesn't that recommend him?' replied Elinor. 'Doesn't it highlight his generosity, his kindness?'

'Yes, but—'

'And as for him having no understanding, I find him highly educated in all the arts, with a love of books and a lively imagination.'

'I didn't say I didn't *like* him,' said Marianne, sensing her sister's irritation. 'He's just not . . . the perfect specimen I imagined you with. Though I suppose no man may be. And of course, if you love him, I shall love him.'

Elinor paled. 'I didn't say I *loved* him.'

'Well, what then?'

'I . . .' – she searched for the word and plucked it like a plum, albeit a small one – 'esteem him.'

' "Esteem" him?'

'Yes, I like him, I don't deny it.'

' "Esteem"?' repeated Marianne. ' "Like"? These are cold-hearted words – no, worse, it's as if you're ashamed of even having feelings at all!'

Elinor blushed. 'We cannot all be as passionate in our language as you, dear Marianne. And besides, I have no proof of his feelings for me, not yet.' She thought for a moment. 'I mean, I sense he feels the same, but even if he were inclined, he is by no means independent. I suspect his mother would make it quite difficult for him if he wanted to marry a woman with neither rank nor fortune, which is what we are now, both of us. No,' she added, as if reassuring herself of the rightness of this, 'it's safer this way. Safer to "esteem".'

And safer it was, for, the moment Fanny got wind of the budding 'friendship' between her beloved brother and less-than-beloved sister-in-law, she took great pains to point out to Mrs Dashwood the express demands of her mother, Mrs Ferrars – that Edward should marry a woman of equal or increased status, and woebetide any unsuitable woman who tried to lure him in.

Enraged, but also concerned for her eldest daughter, Mrs Dashwood vowed not to spend a single day longer than necessary under the same roof as this meddling and cruel woman, and to find virtue in one of Elinor's depressing cottages. But living in such proximity to Norland would surely pain all of them – to see their former home so close, and yet so untouchable.

It is no wonder then that, when a letter arrived the very next morning from a distant cousin, Sir John Middleton, offering her a humble cottage on his Devonshire estate – some hundred and more miles away – she grasped the opportunity as if it were a palace.

CHAPTER FOUR

It was with relief, if not something approaching gloating, that Mrs Dashwood informed her stepson and his wife that they would inconvenience them at Norland no longer.

'Where is this cottage?' demanded Fanny, knowing full well where, having been told only a minute previously.

'Devonshire,' replied Mrs Dashwood. 'Barton Park, to be precise.'

'It's terribly far,' said Fanny. 'Too far for most to visit, I should think.'

'Not for our real friends,' replied Mrs Dashwood, with an obvious nod to Edward, whose expression at the dinner table was equal in pallor and shock to Elinor's.

Fanny bristled. 'How many rooms does it have? The girls will have to share, I presume?'

'Only if they choose,' said Mrs Dashwood.

'I don't mind sharing,' replied Margaret, thinking of the secrets to be earwigged if she were in permanent proximity to her sisters.

'Well, let's see, shall we?' said Elinor.

'No room for horses, of course,' said Fanny. 'Henry can have Captain.'

Marianne let out a yelp. 'But he's mine!'

'But you can't possibly stable him now, nor afford a groom. No, best left to Henry.' Fanny smiled at her son, who was oblivious, shovelling in his third helping of pudding.

'When are you leaving?' asked John.

'As soon as we're packed,' said Mrs Dashwood. 'We'll be taking the china, of course, and our linen.'

Fanny stiffened.

'It is ours, by right,' Elinor stated. 'Papa's wishes.'

'Of course,' said Fanny. 'I had planned to replace it all anyway. Most of it's chipped, or threadbare.'

They were nothing of the sort, but neither Elinor nor Mrs Dashwood sought to correct her, instead they delighted silently in the injury, however small, to Fanny's fortune. 'Tom will join us too,' Mrs Dashwood said. 'And Betsy.'

Fanny recovered. 'I wouldn't have it any other way. I am sure I can spare *two* servants, given I have so *many* here.'

Mrs Dashwood smiled. 'You're too kind.'

Her daughters knew Fanny was anything but. However, not one of them said a word, finishing the meal in quiet contemplation of their fast-changing fate: Margaret thinking of the adventures to be had in the woods and the potential pirates on the sea, which was less than a mile from their new home (she had checked); Marianne imagining the suitors she might meet, the parties she might attend, the inspiration in nature she might gain from such a situation; and Elinor telling herself that separation from Edward was inevitable, and for the best, if she thought about it. And, if he visited, well, that was neither here nor there. It did not matter to her.

Well, only a little bit.

CHAPTER FIVE

The Dashwoods' departure the following Tuesday – the first in September – was, however, anything but silent, as Mrs Dashwood was forced to say goodbye to her happy marital home, and the girls to their childhood one.

Marianne was, as ever, the main source of the commotion. 'Oh, dear, dear Norland!' she wailed, as the carriage made its way through the park to the gates. 'You cannot know how much I suffer to leave you!' And on she went, lamenting the trees, the branches, the individual leaves which had given her shade.

'There *will* be trees in Devonshire,' pointed out Elinor.

But at that Marianne wailed louder, the Devonshire trees assumedly not half as expansive, as tall, as green as these beloved ones.

Elinor did not try to comfort her again with words, but took her sister's hand in her own and in the other, her mother's, as they began their long and melancholy way to their new life.

As they approached Barton Park the following morning, though, the spirits of all four were lifted, for who could not be moved by the view across a lush valley, the sparkle of the sea in the distance, the cheery disposition of the villagers going about their daily business, unaware as they were of the Dashwoods' misfortune?

The cottage itself was not to disappoint either. Though it was small, indeed, compared to Norland, and had neither the green shutters, nor the honeysuckle around the door that Marianne had desperately imagined, it did have a neat wicket gate, a perfectly serviceable set of rooms and enough beds for them to accommodate a guest, should one (such as Edward, perhaps) happen to call. Though that did not prevent Mrs Dashwood from immediately imagining improvements and extensions as soon as their income allowed.

'Perhaps in the spring, if I have plenty of money, which I daresay I shall, I may think about building. Imagine the parties we could give, if only the parlours were joined!'

'Perhaps,' agreed Elinor, knowing full well, as did Mrs Dashwood, that their fortune was as fictitious as unicorns. But, despite this, she joined in the raptures as the family took in their new home.

At that very moment, it was bathed in late summer sun, turning it the colour of honey, and set about with charming plants still in full leaf. Of course, not one of them wondered for a moment how cold it might plummet to in midwinter, how isolated they might become. No, right now, Barton

Cottage had proved an excellent prospect, and they felt indebted to Mrs Dashwood's cousin, Sir John, for his generosity.

'Will we meet him soon?' asked Margaret as she unpacked her precious treasure – a novel involving pirates (as usual), a lucky rabbit's foot (that Marianne could not bear to look upon without imagining the poor creature that died to make it) and a fir cone.

'Soon,' confirmed her mother, busy with linen.

'Careful!' called Marianne, who was occupied ensuring her piano was positioned just where she wanted it, a not entirely easy matter for Tom and his assistant from the village, given how much furniture was already taking up space, and how little room there was to manoeuvre.

'Delivery for Mrs Dashwood,' came another call from the door.

Elinor went to fetch it, since her mother was occupied with soothing Marianne, and was surprised to discover not the postman, but none other than Sir John himself.

'I do hope I'm not intruding,' he bellowed. 'But I did want to see you were settled in.'

'Well, not quite,' said Elinor truthfully, 'but I'm sure it won't take long.'

'Until then, you must dine with us every night.'

'Oh, we couldn't,' began Mrs Dashwood, who, alerted to a cacophony louder than Marianne's, had rushed to greet her cousin.

'I insist!' asserted Sir John loudly, so that neither Mrs Dashwood nor Elinor could bring themselves to deny him. 'Besides, Lady Middleton is so very keen to meet you.'

'Oh, well . . .'

'Good, good!' Sir John agreed. 'I'll send something on as well. To keep you going until then.'

'Oh, nothing too big,' pleaded Elinor.

'Just a mere trifle,' Sir John insisted again (he was a very insistent man, as so many are).

It was not, of course, a mere trifle, but rather, a large basket of fruit and vegetables from Barton Park's own orchards and kitchen garden, followed in less than an hour by a brace of pheasants.

'Paupers,' laughed Elinor, shaking her head as she recalled Marianne's past comment.

But Marianne didn't hear her — she was too busy on her well-placed piano, lost in the lilt of the music (which, to her relief, sounded the same in Devonshire as it had in Sussex), her fingers dancing in and out of the bright slice of country sunlight that fell on the keys.

CHAPTER SIX

Sir John and Lady Middleton complemented each other well: where he was loud and brash, she was a woman of few words. Where he liked only to hunt, she liked only to dote on their four children. Where he loved nothing more than to host extravagant parties, she prided herself on the elegance of the table settings. A good thing too, as Barton Park – a mere half a mile from the cottage – was rarely without several guests.

At the Dashwoods' first visit, there were, however, only two.

After Sir John had greeted the women loudly and enthusiastically, he lowered his tone to apologise. He had, he told them, tried to muster up some others from the neighbourhood, but at such short notice everyone was otherwise engaged. So they would have to do with one Colonel Brandon, who was sadly neither very young, nor a party sort, and Lady Middleton's mother, Mrs Jennings, who would likely make up for Colonel Brandon's lack of gaiety, as partying was practically her profession.

Sir John was not wrong. Colonel Brandon was a silent and serious man, and Mrs Jennings, despite her age, quite the life and soul of this and every party from Devonshire to Dulwich, from where she brought all manner of gossip. But whatever their misgivings, the Dashwoods warmed to both (if only to spite Lady Middleton, who had rather too much in common with Fanny Dashwood) and enjoyed a splendid evening. Marianne, most of all, who discovered Lady Middleton's long-abandoned piano, and set about playing the sheet music that had sat patiently awaiting this day for more than a decade.

While Mrs Dashwood clapped, and Mrs Jennings and Sir John (two peas in a pod) cheered, Elinor noticed that Colonel Brandon sat in silence – entranced by the music or, perhaps, its player.

For better or worse, Elinor was not the only one to catch sight of this.

Mrs Jennings, having seen both of her daughters successfully married, now devoted her spare time to imagining matches between every eligible gentleman and lady. She had, she claimed, quite an excellent skill at prediction and, mark her words, Colonel Brandon and Marianne were meant to be!

She told Marianne later, when visiting the Dashwood's cottage, that she had seen it from the very moment he had watched her at the piano, and hadn't she noted how he always begged her to play after that? He was evidently in love! And what a match it would be, seeing as he was rich, and she was pretty.

Marianne, however, was far from convinced.

'But surely you jest?' she ventured.

Mrs Jennings assured her she never jested, not when it came to matters as serious as those of the heart, and that this was a match – and a serious one.

'But he's ancient!' Marianne railed.

Mrs Dashwood bristled. 'He's only five years younger than I am.'

'Exactly,' said Marianne. 'Old enough to be my father. And even if he was once capable of passion, he must surely have outlived that possibility now. Didn't you hear him complain about his rheumatism? Isn't that the first sign of getting old?'

'I suppose you think I'm lucky to be alive at all then,' said Mrs Dashwood, feeling very much withered, at least under her daughter's critical gaze.

'I didn't say he was about to die,' declared Marianne, missing the point. 'But he's still too old to marry. At least for me.'

'If he were about to die, you'd probably want him,' said Margaret, with rather more insight than was warranted in one so young.

'The quick pulse of the fever,' agreed Elinor, her mind at one with her sister's. 'The romance of the flushed cheek.'

Marianne rolled her eyes. 'He talked about flannel waistcoats. Flannel waistcoats! That's precisely the kind of thing old men wear. Besides, he's already had one attachment, and you know very well I cannot entertain the possibility that a heart can love twice.'

Elinor protested again and at length, as did her mother (who, of course, was Henry Dashwood's second 'attachment') and Mrs Jennings (who believed in any and all attachments), but though Marianne would admit to his kindness and taste (he liked her music after all), she could not and would not admit he might be a match.

'Besides,' she said to her mother, once Mrs Jennings had gone back to Barton Park and Elinor to bed, 'it's Edward Ferrars you should be thinking about. Where on earth is he?'

Where indeed? For the Dashwoods had been at Barton Cottage for weeks now, with no word from him at all.

'What if he's ill?' imagined Marianne. 'Dying, even?'

'It will be nothing of the sort,' said Mrs Dashwood. 'I didn't expect him so soon, anyway. He's a busy man. A very busy man.'

Or so she told herself. Just as she told herself that although he had not made his intentions regarding Elinor entirely clear, and his goodbye to her was perhaps more of the brotherly kind, their match, at least, was as good as made.

CHAPTER SEVEN

The Dashwoods had been settled at Barton Cottage for more than a month, when another gentleman (if he can be called that), and a rival to the Colonel, was introduced into their increasing circle. This time, however, the occasion was not a party, but something rather more perilous.

With autumn upon them, the weather was on the turn, but this did not stop Marianne taking daily walks down to the estuary or up on to the moor. It was there, she claimed, that her passions were at their highest, surrounded by powerful nature. Plus, she had seen a rather fancy mansion at Allenham and had taken to spending swathes of time imagining who might live in it.

'Those clouds look powerful enough,' said Mrs Dashwood, as Marianne buttoned her cloak, and bustled Margaret into her boots. 'Are you sure the two of you should be going out?'

'I welcome the rain,' replied Marianne, as Mrs Dashwood had feared she might. 'The tender drops, the wash of it all. It is most mesmerising!'

Neither Mrs Dashwood nor Elinor, who had tried warnings of her own, bothered to say anything further, for there was no telling Marianne what to do at the best of times. And so, with the clouds bunched blackly on the horizon and the tang of a storm on the sea air, the younger sisters set off for the hills.

'What wonder!' called Marianne, as the wind whipped their faces. 'There is nothing in the world better than this!'

'Are you sure this is sensible?' asked Margaret,

who, despite her sense of adventure, was none too keen on the darkening sky. 'I think it would be better to head back.'

'Nonsense!' replied Marianne, who had no time for sense, only beauty. 'We shall walk for at least two hours. I pity Elinor for missing it.'

And on they marched, until, less than twenty minutes later, the full force of rain pelted them in their faces and, with no shelter in sight, they were forced to abandon the plan and head back at speed – not an easy task given the slope of the hill and its increasing slickness.

'Wait for me!' called Margaret as Marianne ran ahead.

She needn't have asked, for no sooner had she spoken than Marianne tripped and tumbled, falling several feet down a steep ravine.

'Marianne!' wailed Margaret. 'Are you all right? Shall I fetch help?'

'Allow me,' came a voice.

Margaret turned and, to her surprise, found herself confronted by quite the most dashing man she had seen in her life.

'Here,' he said, handing Margaret his gun – a hunter, then, so definitely dashing. And with that, he descended the perilous slope with ease, picked up Marianne, who made not a murmur of protest, and carried her over his shoulder, all the way back to Barton Cottage, the gobsmacked Margaret scampering in his wake.

Mrs Dashwood and Elinor were no less entranced. As the group entered, they both stood, their mouths slightly agape. Of course, any act of kindness to Marianne would have been greeted with gratitude, but something about his handsome face, his impeccable manners, the cut of his cloak, made it seem all the more . . . generous, no . . . gallant.

'Oh, thank you!' cried Mrs Dashwood. 'Please, do sit down. You must be exhausted.'

'That's too kind,' said the gentleman. 'But I'm wet through and would hate to soak your chaise. Perhaps I may call tomorrow, though. To check on your daughter's health – or is she your sister?'

'Oh!' Mrs Dashwood giggled. 'My daughter, of course. And yes, please do, Mr . . .?'

'Willoughby,' he finished for her. 'Willoughby of Allenham.'

'Willoughby,' repeated Marianne to herself as she settled into bed that evening. A fine name for a fine man. In fact, one might say, he was equal to any hero in a storybook, to any leading man she had ever conjured up for herself. He was dashing, handsome, and he was connected to the manor she had admired. Perhaps, she imagined, even its heir.

Yes, Willoughby was the one for her. Not old Colonel Brandon with his rheumatism and flannel waistcoats, but young and thrusting Willoughby in his shooting coat: the uniform, surely, of the very best of men.

CHAPTER EIGHT

By the next morning, not only were all four Dashwoods smitten with the enigmatic Willoughby, he was also a good deal less mysterious, as Mrs Dashwood and Marianne had made lengthy enquiries as to his character from Sir John.

'Willoughby?' barked Sir John (who was as prone to barking as he was to bellowing). 'Is he here? Oh, splendid. A finer man you'll not find for miles.'

'You know him, then?' said Mrs Dashwood.

'Know him? Why, of course. I hunt with him.'

'And what is he . . . like?' asked Marianne.

'Like?' repeated Sir John. 'Why, there's no

bolder rider in the country. And unstoppable, too – he danced from eight until four in the morning at our Christmas do, I recall, then still got up to hunt the following day.'

That was not quite what Marianne had meant, but she took it as a good sign nonetheless.

'Heir to Allenham Manor, of course,' continued Sir John. 'Comes down every year to see his sick aunt. Devoted, he is. And an estate of his own in Somerset – Combe Park, I believe.'

Now that was more like it.

'Yes,' mused Sir John. 'Quite a catch, if you can get him.'

Mrs Dashwood went red. 'None of my daughters have been brought up to "catch" a man,' she flustered. 'It's the men that will need to do the catching.'

Marianne nodded, as was proper, but in her mind, Willoughby's line was already cast and she, the tender young salmon, was well and truly hooked. She could barely breathe as she awaited his call that afternoon, and when she saw him approach up the lane, she arranged herself on the chaise in as attractive a manner as she could imagine.

'Miss Dashwood.' He bowed as he greeted her. 'You are much better, I see.'

'Much,' managed Marianne. 'Quite well, in fact.'

Never better, thought Elinor to herself, as she observed her sister's fluttering eyelashes, the enthusiasm with which she went on to entertain Willoughby with talk of her very favourite novelists ('Mine too, what luck!') and music ('Why, Marianne, you are quite right, the Vivaldi is far superior to the Bach!'). In fact, there was not one matter on which they disagreed and Elinor was forced to admit this might be the match for Marianne after all. Pity pricked her heart at the thought of poor Colonel Brandon.

For his part, Willoughby showed every sign of being as smitten as her sister.

He called every day, and every day the pair engaged in their shared delights – music and books – as well as countless walks (weather permitting) once she was well enough.

'He's perfect,' declared Marianne.

'Perfect?' repeated Elinor. 'I thought you said

you would never find such a man?'

'Oh, I was young then,' said Marianne, forgetting it was mere weeks ago. 'A flibbertigibbet. Now I am older and wiser to the world, and I know him to be the very best in it.'

Something Willoughby, no doubt, would have agreed with. He certainly did not have high regard for his rival, the Colonel.

'Brandon is the kind of man,' said Willoughby one day, 'that everyone speaks well of, but nobody cares about. He is,' he continued, warming to his theme, 'the kind of man everyone is happy to see but can't be bothered to talk to.'

'That is rather unfair,' said Elinor carefully. 'I talk to him at length.'

'Well, of course you would,' said Marianne. 'Because you feel pity for him, as you would for an injured puppy.'

'I . . .' But Elinor was forced to admit to herself that pity him she did. Even so, she admired him too. 'He has travelled the world,' she ventured. 'He is a mine of information, and kind with it.'

'I suppose he's told you the East Indies are hot and mosquitoes are bothersome,' said an unusually sarcastic Marianne, to great roars from Willoughby.

'What is it you so dislike about him?' demanded Elinor.

'I never said I disliked him,' said Willoughby. 'For what is there to dislike in one so dull?'

Marianne giggled.

Elinor sighed. There was no doubt about it now: her sister was caught, good and proper, and all that remained was actual engagement, which she assumed would be announced any day.

CHAPTER NINE

Before they moved to Barton Cottage, the Dashwoods couldn't possibly have imagined the number of luncheons and picnics and parties they would end up attending. And at all of them was the devoted Willoughby.

While the engagement itself was still not official, his public admiration of Marianne was exactly calculated to give the impression that the announcement would be soon. They were inseparable, or so it seemed to Elinor, and demonstrative in their affection – a fact that bothered her greatly.

'Do you not think you might be a little less . . . showy about it?' she suggested.

'What on earth for?' demanded Marianne. 'Why should we pretend to not adore each other? And anyway, how could we possibly do such a thing, given how strongly we feel?'

'It's just . . . not done,' managed Elinor.

Marianne snorted. 'Not done? We can't all pretend to have hearts of ice. And anyway, Mama doesn't seem to mind.'

Mrs Dashwood did not mind, for her daughter was evidently enraptured with the man. Everything Willoughby did was right; everything he said was clever or hilarious. When they played cards, he would lose deliberately so that Marianne could win. When they danced, they danced only with each other. Yes, coming to Barton Park had been the making of the girl.

If only the same could be said of her older sister.

Elinor, of course, had no such attachment to occupy her. Her heart was still somewhere between there and Norland, in the pocket of Mr Edward Ferrars, not that she could possibly admit such a thing, not even to herself. Instead she would occupy her mind listening to Mrs Jennings's endless tattling – her life history, the ins and outs of her late husband's illnesses, his last words before he died. Really, there was no subject off limits, it seemed. It was with relief when she found herself in the company of Colonel Brandon, whose seriousness was almost soothing, even if his subject was, more often than not, Marianne.

'Your sister does not believe in second attachments then,' he ventured one evening.

Elinor shook her head. 'She's a romantic,' she told him. 'She does not believe it possible a heart can love with such strength more than once. She'll grow out of it, perhaps. With age comes wisdom.'

'Though there is something to be admired in such youthful prejudice,' said the Colonel, his eyes fixed on Marianne (really, he was a lost cause).

'Is there no sway at all?' he asked then, turning to Elinor. 'Are those who have been jilted, or . . . prevented in some way from marriage to be thought incapable of loving again?'

'I honestly don't think she makes any exceptions,' said Elinor. 'I'm sorry.'

'No, quite right,' said the Colonel. 'Her opinion is charming, in any case. I once knew a girl much like her – passionate, angry when challenged – only, a series of unfortunate events meant she was forced to change, forced to—'

At that he stopped, as if realising he had already said too much.

Elinor, being Elinor, did not push him to finish his story. Only wondered at the unhappy ending. And wondered too, if circumstances had been different, it might have been the Colonel twirling Marianne round the floor as they danced their third gavotte of the evening, rather than Willoughby, who – it was evident – had had one too many sherries.

CHAPTER TEN

The following morning, though an engagement ring was still very much missing from Marianne's finger, Willoughby had at least presented her with evidence of his wealth. He had, she told her sisters excitedly, given her a horse!

'He bred it himself!' she exclaimed. 'A thoroughbred cross. Exactly calculated to carry a woman!'

'But aren't some women larger than others?' asked Margaret, who had a point.

'Haven't you got piano to practise?' demanded Marianne, then turned back to her older sister, who would surely embrace this news. 'Can you believe it? A horse!'

Elinor could quite easily believe it.

'Of course, we'll need to build a stable. And get another horse to keep it company. And probably a servant to ride that. But a horse! Just think of it.'

Elinor did think of it, but Marianne's excitement was to be dashed. 'And how on earth will we pay for it?' she asked. 'Or for the stable, and the other horse and the servant?'

'Oh,' said Marianne.

'Oh, indeed.'

'But . . . it wouldn't be *too* expensive, I don't think. Any old pony would do for the servant. And' – she scrabbled for something more persuasive – 'you could ride it too!'

A different tack was clearly needed. 'Don't you think,' began Elinor delicately, 'that it's a bit much accepting such a . . . generous gift from someone you hardly know?'

'Hardly know? Why, I know him better than

anyone in the world, except you, Margaret and Mama, of course.'

'But you only met him a matter of weeks ago.'

'Time is nothing when it comes to affairs of the heart. And anyway, I've known my stepbrother all my life, yet could not tell you a single intimate thing about him, other than his name is John and he's married to a harridan. Whereas I know hundreds of things about Willoughby. Everything, in fact.'

Everything? Elinor doubted that, but did not say so. Instead, she went back to worrying about how much money their poor mother would have to shell out, painting such a dismal picture that in the end, Marianne gave in and agreed gloomily that she would tell Willoughby the horse was off.

The gloom, however, was short-lived. For Willoughby simply told her that Queen Mab (for that was the horse's name) would be ready and waiting, as soon as she left Barton for a more 'lasting establishment'.

Now, to anyone else's ears, certainly Elinor's, that could have meant anything – a move for the whole family, for example, to a permanent residence; they could not stay at the cottage rent-free for ever, of course. But in Marianne's vivid imagination, as well as her mother's (who happened to be listening in) that 'lasting establishment' was Allenham or Combe Park. Or, preferably, both. Why, she could ride between them!

And that was not the only evidence of engagement. Later that afternoon, Margaret burst in on Elinor, with a secret so big she could not be expected to contain it for a second.

'He's going to marry her soon!' she cried.

Elinor looked up from her sketching. 'You've been saying that every day since they met.'

'But he has a lock of her hair!'

Elinor paused. If it were true, this would be evidence indeed. 'Are you sure? It could be . . . someone else's.'

'It's Marianne's. I saw him snip it himself. Then he kissed it and folded it up in a piece of white paper and put it in his pocketbook.'

Elinor could no longer doubt it: Marianne was to be wed. While she, the elder, was further from love than ever.

And so too was poor Colonel Brandon.

CHAPTER ELEVEN

Elinor's silence about her own passions did not stop Mrs Jennings endlessly enquiring after them. Nor did it stop Margaret, whose ability to keep secrets was becoming more and more questionable.

'She does like someone,' Margaret blurted after the latest round of interrogation at Barton Park. 'But I'm not allowed to tell, am I, Elinor?'

Elinor reddened at even the suggestion. 'I don't know what you mean. You must be imagining things again.'

'I didn't imagine anything,' said Margaret, quite put out at the accusation. 'You told me yourself.'

Mrs Jennings squawked with laughter and begged Margaret to tell her his name.

'I can't say his name,' said Margaret. 'But I can say it begins with an "F".'

'Oh, a game!' said Mrs Jennings. 'I love a game. Is it Franklin? No, wait, I have it: Fazackerley! There's a very eligible Fazackerley just outside Trowbridge.'

'No and no!' replied Margaret. 'Try again.'

'Margaret,' warned Elinor. 'You know very well this man doesn't exist.'

'That's odd,' said Margaret. 'Because I am sure I met him, and his name definitely began with an "F".'

Elinor was about to protest again when, having said nothing for what seemed like weeks, Lady Middleton (who did not like games of any kind) announced it was raining, and several of the party rushed to the window to look.

Willoughby sat back down, smiling like the cat who had the cream. 'All the better for staying in and listening to your piano playing,' he told Marianne.

Colonel Brandon frowned. 'It will clear by the morning,' he said, with some finality. 'And then perhaps we can all go out. I know a fine place for a picnic, and a boat trip.'

'A boat!' exclaimed Marianne.

Willoughby scowled, but briefly. 'A boat, how wonderful. Well *we* will be delighted to accompany you.'

And so, the outing was set for the morning. An outing Elinor had serious doubts about, given the season – it was almost November, after all. But she did not voice anything, merely thanked the Lord that everyone's attention was no longer on that wretched guessing game.

At least for now.

CHAPTER TWELVE

In the event, the picnic did
not pan out as planned.

By ten in the morning,
everyone was assembled at
Barton Park, but at the last minute,
Colonel Brandon received a
message, which must have
contained grave news indeed,
for, on reading it, he turned
white and remained silent for
several moments.

'Is it bad news?' asked
Mrs Jennings, with what

may have sounded to some like a hint of hope in her voice.

The Colonel said it was not.

'Is it from your sister in France?' tried Mrs Jennings. 'Is she dying?'

'No.'

'Or is your cousin to be married?'

The Colonel could bear it no longer. 'I am to go to London,' he announced. 'I'm sorry, but it cannot be helped. The outing will have to be postponed.'

'To London?' demanded Mrs Jennings. 'What on earth for? What is there to do in London at this time of year?'

'I think he just cannot bear other people having fun,' suggested Willoughby, with what could only be described as a sneer. 'He probably wrote the letter himself.'

'Probably,' agreed Marianne, evidently desperate to side with her suitor.

'I'm sorry,' repeated the Colonel. 'But, as I say' – he looked pointedly at Willoughby – 'nothing can be done.'

'When will you back?' asked Elinor. 'Soon, I hope.'

'I honestly don't know,' replied Colonel Brandon. 'It's not . . . up to me.'

'Such a shame,' said Elinor.

The Colonel nodded in thanks and then was gone.

'Fishy,' said Sir John.

'Indeed,' agreed Mrs Jennings.

'If he's not back by the end of the week, I'll go after him and find out what's going on.'

'Oh, do!' she replied.

'Obviously something he's ashamed of.'

'Obviously. I'd wager it's Miss Williams.'

'Miss Williams?' asked Margaret.

'Oh, I should not say!' said Mrs Jennings, knowing full well she would, and any moment. 'But she's his . . . well, his *daughter*!'

Elinor could hardly believe it. A daughter? What secrets the poor Colonel must bear on his own. She turned to gauge her sister's reaction, and realised Marianne was, in fact, missing.

'Where's Marianne?' she asked.

'Oh, with Willoughby, I assume,' said Mrs Jennings. 'Quite the lovebirds, aren't they? Any day, mark my words, any day!'

Marianne was indeed with Willoughby. And where? Only gallivanting around the countryside in his carriage, stopping to view Allenham and all its rooms, as if she were Lady of the Manor already.

'Where?' demanded Elinor, after the couple had returned several hours later.

'I told you. Honestly, Elinor, you should have seen the bedrooms!'

'Bedrooms?' Elinor was aghast. 'Was his aunt aware of this?'

'No, why should she be? She's ill.'

'So, you were entirely alone with him? In the bedroom?'

'Yes.'

Elinor was exasperated. 'Can you not see how this looks?'

'How does it look?'

'So . . .' What word summed up this sort of behaviour in the absence of an actual engagement, if not marriage itself? Oh, yes, that was it, 'improper,' she finished.

'Improper? Nonsense,' replied Marianne. 'If it had been improper I would have felt it, and I felt nothing but joy. Oh, you should have seen it! The sitting room upstairs is almost perfect. I mean, it will only take a few hundred pounds for some new furniture – the current pieces are dreadfully drab – but then . . . exquisite!'

And on Marianne would go, so that Colonel Brandon's departure was completely forgotten, in favour of curtains and carpet and gardens.

CHAPTER THIRTEEN

While Marianne was easily distracted, Mrs Jennings was a dog with a bone, refusing to drop the subject of Colonel Brandon's disappearance for a single moment.

'Such melancholy!' she declared to anyone who would listen. 'It must be his sister. Or, no, wait, it will be Miss Williams, I am sure of it.' She paused for breath, and sherry. 'Or, I daresay his estate at Delaford is in trouble. His fortune may be squandered, or gone!'

Elinor did not reply, for no reply was necessary. And besides, she had concerns of her own: why had Marianne and Willoughby not announced their engagement? If Margaret were to be believed, he had a lock of her hair. Then there was the business with the horse, and the visit to Allenham. Why take her there, if not to show her her future home?

Perhaps, she thought, *he couldn't afford it.* Oh, he had his estate, but, according to Sir John, that only brought him six or seven hundred a year, and Willoughby clearly spent a good deal more than that, what with his partying and hunting.

But if his reasons were not clear, his intentions regarding Marianne, as well as his adoration of all

the Dashwoods, seemed to be. He was certainly always present, treating the cottage as if it were his own home.

'Perfect,' he declared, putting his feet up on a stool. 'So modest, and yet, yes, perfect.'

'Do you think so?' asked Mrs Dashwood in all earnestness. 'Because I was thinking of some improvements in the spring. Extending, adding rooms – if we can afford it, of course.'

'Improvements?' he cried, almost affronted. 'I will not hear of it. In fact, I cannot hear of it, for how could one improve on perfection? I hope you stay poor for ever, rather than change this mansion.'

'Mansion?' said Mrs Dashwood, looking at the whitewashed walls and lumpy wooden furniture.

'More than a mansion: a palace,' he elaborated. 'In fact, if I had the money, I would knock down my own manor and build a copy of Barton Cottage in its place!'

Mrs Dashwood beamed, as did Marianne. And their smiles were about to widen further.

'I must be away,' said Willoughby then. 'But I would like to call on you all tomorrow, if I may, at four.'

'At four,' agreed Marianne quickly. For this was surely it: his marriage proposal was imminent. Oh, tomorrow would be a happy day!

Yes, everything would be settled tomorrow.

CHAPTER FOURTEEN

Of course, in her excitement, Marianne had completely forgotten the Dashwoods were to be at Barton Park in the afternoon – at the very moment Mr Willoughby was due to return.

'But they won't even notice if I'm not there,' she pleaded.

'Oh, I think you do yourself a disservice,' said Elinor. 'How could they possibly not notice the sudden peace?'

Marianne scowled. 'Anyway, I have . . . things to do and . . . a bit of a stomach ache. Mama, *please* let me stay.'

'Of course,' said Mrs Dashwood, without

further interrogation, and to Elinor's surprise. 'Well, obviously he's arranged to speak to her privately first,' she explained to her daughters, once they were off to the Middletons. 'We'll join them as soon as politeness allows.'

More like if we can ever get away from Mrs Jennings, thought Elinor, but, as ever, she kept her thoughts to herself, and found that she was secretly pleased for her sister. This was the match Marianne so wanted, after all. They were 'destined to be', she had declared. Soulmates.

Well, at four o'clock their destiny would be sealed, the date set, perhaps, and wedding bells would ring in Allenham parish before the year was out. Or so Elinor assured herself, as they sat through luncheon, and then several games of cards, and at least an hour of Mrs Jennings's complaining about her painful feet.

'Shouldn't we be going?' Elinor suggested, as the clock ticked close to quarter to four.

'Oh, my heavens,' exclaimed Mrs Dashwood, looking up. 'Is that the time?'

And, ignoring Sir John's pleas for another game, and Mrs Jennings' pleas to listen to her latest theories on the Colonel's mysterious disappearance, the women departed, Margaret in hot pursuit.

'We'll be late!' cried Mrs Dashwood, hanging on to her hat.

'Late for what?' asked Margaret, who was not privy to her mother and sisters' assumptions.

'It won't matter anyway,' said a breathless Elinor. 'He'll ask, whether we're there or not. It's not as if he can get Papa's permission.'

'What won't matter?' begged Margaret, as they threw open the front door.

'Nothing! Just—' But if Elinor were about to admit anything, it was soon swallowed down, for there in front of her was her sister. But not the beaming bride-to-be she had expected, rather a tear-stained maiden, who ran sobbing to her room.

'Marianne?' said Mrs Dashwood, then turning to Willoughby, who stood sheepishly in the hallway. 'Whatever has happened? Is she ill?'

'I hope not,' he said. 'I think rather it is that . . . I have to leave, you see. For London.'

'London?' she repeated. 'Again?'

'Is it to see Colonel Brandon?' asked Margaret.

Hardly, thought Elinor.

'My aunt insists,' explained Willoughby, though it barely threw any light on the matter.

'But you will be back soon?' Elinor suggested.

Willoughby paused. 'No, I . . . only visit my aunt once a year.'

Elinor could hardly believe what she was hearing.

Nor could Mrs Dashwood. 'But you could visit us here instead?' she offered. 'You are always welcome.'

'That's very kind,' Willoughby said stiffly. 'But I don't think my . . . business will allow it.'

'Oh!' Mrs Dashwood looked set to follow her daughter in weeping.

'I should go,' said Willoughby. 'It is foolish to drag this out. Torment for me, even.'

And, bowing briefly, he departed, leaving three Dashwoods open-mouthed in the hallway, and one upstairs with her head buried in her pillow.

★ ★ ★

With her mother upstairs trying to get the truth from Marianne, Elinor stood in silence trying to work it out for herself. She veered between thinking Willoughby had never been serious about her sister at all and guessing the pair had had some terrible argument; Marianne's face had certainly suggested the latter. But what quarrel could there have been when their love was so great?

Mrs Dashwood was unable to shed any light when she returned from Marianne's bedside. 'Poor Willoughby,' she lamented. 'He seemed so heavy-hearted.'

Elinor did not think Willoughby was their main concern, given Marianne's audible sobbing. But she agreed his behaviour was certainly out of character. 'It is all very strange,' she added.

'Perhaps his aunt found out about Marianne?' suggested Mrs Dashwood. 'And she doesn't approve and has sent him away as a distraction!'

She sounded like Mrs Jennings. 'But wouldn't he object?' said Elinor.

'Oh, but he will know that she doesn't approve and so has agreed merely in order to buy time! Yes, that will be it!'

Even if Mrs Dashwood's version of the story were right (and what other possibility was there?), the situation, Elinor felt, hardly warranted dancing with glee, as her mother seemed to be doing. And then there was the matter of the engagement, or rather the *lack* of it.

'What do you mean, no evidence?' demanded Mrs Dashwood when Elinor brought it up. 'I have seen his affection with my own two eyes.'

'And I,' agreed Elinor. 'But no evidence of his commitment.' The lock of hair was no ring, after all.

'Then why would he shower her with love? Why spend every waking moment in her company? You must think awfully of him if you think him capable of such pretence.'

'No!' Elinor replied. 'I don't believe him a deceitful man.' Or did she? No, she must not, for Marianne's sake. 'I just . . . No, you're right. It is surely down to his aunt. And he must be as devastated as Marianne. Poor man.'

Poor man indeed, if Marianne was anything to go by. For though she did come down at dinner-time, she spoke not a word, ate not a morsel, and when her mother tried to pat her hand in comfort, she burst into tears again and fled from the room.

CHAPTER FIFTEEN

Marianne would never have forgiven herself if she had slept that first night after Willoughby's departure. Sorrow was to be wallowed in, after all, and how would it have looked had she gone down to breakfast looking well-rested? But she needn't have worried, there was no chance of even a wink. Instead, she tossed and turned and sobbed and wailed and when she did come down in the morning, again refused to speak or eat. Instead, she went straight out to wander around the village remembering the special places Willoughby had taken her, and promptly began to cry all over again.

Marianne did this the next day and the next. In the evenings she played every song Willoughby had ever sung and read only books that she and Willoughby had discussed, and so the melancholy went on for days, with no word at all from the man himself.

'Surely he must write?' said Elinor, flinching as she realised there had been no letter from Edward Ferrars either, and for far longer.

Her mother did not notice, in any case, being far too busy conjuring up theories of her own to explain the situation. 'It will be because he knows Sir John may intercept the post and the aunt will find out!'

'Perhaps,' said Elinor.

'Definitely,' decided Mrs Dashwood. And, noting Marianne's slightly improved disposition that morning – she had eaten an egg, and a slice of bread – that was the last time either of them mentioned his name for weeks.

★ ★ ★

As the autumn days passed, Marianne continued to improve to the point where, instead of stalking Allenham alone, she joined her sisters on a stroll up the hill. Here, they stopped to admire the view that they now called home: the cottage, the park, the wide estuary, set into woods like a sliver of silver foil. And there, along the path, something else; something moving.

'A horse!' said Margaret.

'A man on a horse,' elaborated Elinor.

'Willoughby!' exclaimed Marianne.

'Really?' questioned Elinor, for the figure was too faint to make out in detail; only the riding position gave away it was a male.

'I know it!' Marianne declared, and ran towards him, her sisters calling after her. Not that Marianne would listen even if she could hear, her ears were only for the voice of Willoughby, which would be hers any moment. Any moment—

She stopped, squinted, and felt her heart sink.

While at the same time, her elder sister's leapt. It was not Willoughby. But it was a man indeed. One beginning with 'F'.

It was, of course, Edward Ferrars.

'Where have you been?' cried Margaret. 'We thought you may be dead!'

'I ... no, not dead,' replied Edward. 'In

London. And then Devonshire.'

'But only *just* in Devonshire, surely,' suggested Elinor, greeting him more formally with her outstretched hand.

'A fortnight,' he replied.

A fortnight? Elinor's insides flipped. Now she understood a little how Marianne felt – all that turmoil. 'But you didn't call sooner?' she asked.

Edward blushed, evidently distressed at this oversight. 'I was in Plymouth . . . with friends.'

'Well, you're here now,' said Elinor, mustering.

'And in such wonderful company,' he replied. 'And a wonderful place.'

'Hardly,' said Marianne, sulkily. 'It is a painful place. Terribly painful.'

'I'll explain later,' said Elinor. 'Come. Mama will be delighted.'

And, she too. Why, her heart was almost – was it? Yes! – dancing as she led him up the path to the cottage.

CHAPTER SIXTEEN

'It's not exactly a palace,' Elinor said as they entered Barton Cottage, almost wincing as she felt the sharp needle of shame. For surely Edward couldn't fail to see how far down the Dashwoods had tumbled since their Norland days?

But Edward smiled. 'Well, I'm not exactly a prince,' he said, dispelling her doubts like confetti on the wind.

'Edward?' checked Mrs Dashwood, as her visitor approached. 'Is that you?'

'I believe it is,' said Edward, his normally awkward manner impossible in the face of such a welcome. 'Or, I was this morning.'

'How lucky we are!' she cried, not put out for a moment that it wasn't Willoughby in front of her.

'No, I'm the lucky one,' said Edward quietly, and went on to say it twice more as he was taken around the house and garden and shown Elinor's sketches of both.

But for all his joy at arriving, by dinner his spirits seemed to have sunk a little, and everyone saw it.

'How is your mother?' said Mrs Dashwood, sensing this might be the source of his sorrow. 'Is she still convinced you are to be an MP?'

'Thankfully not,' admitted Edward. 'She has finally seen what I have known all along: I have no talent for speeches. And yet . . . she is still determined I shall be famous, and rich besides.'

'And how do you intend to do that?' asked Mrs Dashwood.

'I don't,' said Edward frankly. 'I have no desire for money or grandeur.'

'Quite right,' agreed Marianne. 'Neither are the source of happiness.'

Elinor smiled. 'Grandeur, no. But enough money is surely part of it?'

'Only if there is nothing else to make one happy,' replied Marianne. 'For my part, I barely require any.'

'Oh, really?' said Elinor. 'And how much is barely any?'

Marianne pondered. 'Oh, only two thousand a year. No more than that.'

'Two thousand a year?' Elinor laughed. 'You do remember that we have only one thousand?'

Marianne pulled a face. 'But two thousand is hardly anything. A family can't live on anything less. And it's not like I'm asking for much: only a servant or ten, a carriage, a few good horses.'

'Hardly anything, then.' Elinor looked at Edward, who met her with a smile to match her own.

'I wish someone would give us all a fortune,' said Margaret, with a sigh.

'Oh, yes!' said Marianne.

'Well, we agree on something,' said Elinor.

And so the Dashwoods set about spending their imaginary thousands. Mrs Dashwood would make her improvements to the cottage, Margaret would set off on some kind of ill-advised adventure, and as for the older sisters, a cheerier Edward suggested it would be a happy day for music shops and booksellers, as they could afford to buy the lot.

'You could even pay an author to write whatever you wished,' he told Marianne.

'Oh, no,' she said mysteriously. 'I have other plans.' But on those, she would not be drawn.

'I am glad to see you smile,' said Edward to Elinor. 'You seemed so grave when I arrived.'

'You can talk,' she replied. 'You hardly seem the happiest man alive.'

'No,' he said, his smile fading. 'Perhaps not.'

Elinor felt her own spirits sink slightly. Something had changed in Edward since their joyful days at Norland, and it was not to do with his mother, at least not entirely.

She was trying to stop herself guessing, when Marianne let out a shriek. 'Edward, is that a ring?'

His eyes joined Elinor's and Mrs Dashwood's as they all gazed at his finger, on which was a band of gold and a glass circle containing a lock of hair.

Elinor's heart set to hammering. Whose hair was it? She could hardly ask, could she? How pushy that would seem.

Marianne was not so embarrassed, however. 'I never saw you wear a ring before,' she declared. 'And whose hair is it? Fanny's?'

Edward, redder than ever, looked at Elinor, then nodded quickly. 'Of course, it's my sister's hair.'

Marianne frowned. 'I thought her hair was a shade darker.'

'No, no. It must be the light,' said Edward, catching Elinor's eye again.

But it wasn't the light, Elinor was sure of it. And the colour matched exactly her own. He must have taken it without her knowing, which was rather bold of him. But still, her hair!

She must not let on she knew, though. Not to anyone. Especially not Marianne, whose own match was still somewhat in tatters. She quelled the swell of affection inside her. 'How charming,' she said, nodding at Edward. 'More tea, anyone?'

CHAPTER SEVENTEEN

Edward stayed with the Dashwoods for a week, his spirits lifting until he was almost his old self again. It was clear to everyone that he adored the peace of the country, the plants and the people most of all.

'Must you leave?' begged Elinor. 'You don't even like London.'

'Nor Norland,' admitted Edward. 'But I have to go to one of them.'

'But why?' said Elinor, surprising herself at her insistence.

'I just . . . have to,' he replied. 'I'm sorry.'

Elinor left it there, but her irritation continued long after Edward had departed. Was it his mother wanting to see him? Or stopping him seeing Elinor? *How awful*, she thought, reminded suddenly and uncomfortably of Willoughby and his demanding aunt. Or, more probably, Mrs Ferrars was simply pressing him to better himself in the fame stakes. Well, perhaps, Elinor allowed herself a crumb of comfort, he would win her over. He had seemed so set on something, after all. So . . . determined. And as quickly as they had set in, her doubts were dispelled and she remembered instead their time together – the walks, the talking, the laughter – all proof of his affection for her. And none more so than the ring he wore on his finger containing the lock of her hair.

Over the coming days, Elinor continued to dwell on Edward whenever she was idle, even when she was busy with sewing or sketching she found herself thinking of him and missing him terribly. But she let on nothing of the depth of her feeling to her sisters or mother, did not admit that he consumed her every waking thought. It was just so unlike her. And not at all sensible, she knew. What she needed was some other distraction.

Luckily for Elinor, Sir John and Mrs Jennings were about to provide several.

The first was the arrival of the Palmers.

While Mrs Jennings's youngest and very pregnant daughter, Charlotte – now Mrs Palmer – took after her mother in her enthusiasm of life and delight in discussing it, her husband managed to be as grumpy in thought as his sister-in-law, Lady Middleton. However, he did not share her reluctance in discussing his complaints.

'Your house is quite charming!' declared Mrs Palmer on arriving at Barton Cottage. 'And what a beautiful room.' She turned to her husband. 'Isn't it quite delightful? I would so love a room like this.'

Her husband grunted in obvious denial, and his dissent at everything only got worse as the days went on.

'This weather is disgusting,' he announced, as the Dashwoods sat down to dine at Barton Park. 'It makes everything and everybody miserable.'

'Oh, ignore him,' said Mrs Palmer.

But it was quite hard to do when all he did was bluster and beef.

'And why is there no billiard table? What's a man to do without a billiard table?'

'Isn't he the funniest?' laughed Mrs Palmer.

Elinor nodded kindly, though funny was not the word she would have chosen.

'Of course he's quite exhausted from campaigning for parliament. If you want to be an MP, you have to persuade everyone to like you!'

Neither Elinor nor Marianne believed such a feat possible, though they did not let on for a second.

'And you must both come to Cleveland for Christmas, of course,' rattled on Mrs Palmer. 'You and Marianne. We would so adore it! Wouldn't we, dear?'

Mr Palmer pulled a face. 'I can think of nothing better,' he said in a tone that suggested he'd rather clip his toenails.

Marianne glanced at her sister, the prospect of spending more time with Mr Palmer quite unappealing. Elinor smiled politely. 'I don't think that will be possible,' she said.

'London, then,' said Mrs Palmer. 'We have a wonderful house in Hanover Square. I'm sure I could find you somewhere nearby.'

Elinor saw her sister's eyes light up at this suggestion, evidently forgetting the horror of Mr Palmer, and thinking instead of Willoughby, as she, admittedly, thought of Edward.

But to hire a house, for several weeks? It was impossible. 'I'm sorry—'

'I can chaperone you if Mrs Dashwood cannot accompany you,' said Mrs Palmer. Until the baby comes, of course.'

'It's not that,' said Elinor.

'But—' Marianne started.

'No,' interrupted Elinor decisively. 'It's . . . it cannot be done.'

She looked at Marianne, who scowled, refusing to acknowledge that a long stay in London was really rather beyond their financial means these days.

'Well, Mr Palmer will be most disappointed,' she said, and prodded her husband. 'Won't you?'

'Devastated,' he said flatly.

CHAPTER EIGHTEEN

The Palmers departed Barton Park the next day, but their presence was quickly filled with new guests: two sisters that Mrs Jennings had met in Exeter and was delighted to discover were her distant cousins.

The Misses Steele were both women and both in their twenties, but there the similarities ended. The elder, Nancy, was as plain in face as she was in words, while Lucy was quite the polite beauty.

Where Nancy was effusive, Lucy was reserved; where Nancy's tongue had a habit of running away with her, Lucy kept hers in check; where Nancy didn't much mind everyone knowing their business (as she liked to know everyone else's), Lucy would rather keep some things to trusted company only.

As Elinor would soon find out.

'How are you finding Devonshire?' asked Lucy politely, as they dined at Barton Park one evening.

'I—' began Elinor.

'I bet you were sorry to leave Sussex, though,' interrupted Nancy. 'I heard Norland's prodigious pretty!'

Lucy winced at Nancy's manners. For, while she herself had tried to refine her accent and choose her words carefully, her sister saw no point in such pretension and spoke exactly as she felt, and often. 'Sir John told us,' Lucy said quickly, to dispel the suggestion of gossip. But if she hoped to quiet her sister, it was to be dashed within seconds.

'I think everyone admires it,' said a measured Elinor. 'Though none more than us, perhaps.'

'I bet you had a lot of lovely men there too,' added Nancy. 'I do love lovely men.'

Lucy composed herself. 'I'm sure there are some fine men here.'

'I never said there weren't any,' said Nancy. 'And p'raps the Dashwoods an't interested anyway. Though for my part, I can't bear being without, as long as they dress smart and act nice. There's a Mr Rose in Exeter, for example, dandy as he is handsome in the afternoon, but if you saw him first thing in the morning! Lawks! Though, he's married anyway, more's the pity.'

'Heavens, Nancy!' chided her sister. 'I'm quite sure the Dashwoods will assume you think of nothing but men if you carry on.'

Which indeed, they did. For the very next day,

Nancy brought the subject up again, and in a most alarming manner.

'I hear your sister's getting wed!' she said to Elinor. 'And Sir John says he's ever so handsome and all. Though I 'spect you'll find one as nice soon. Unless' – Nancy nudged Elinor – 'you've already found one!'

'Oh, she has!' said Sir John, who'd been earwigging. 'Begins with an "F".'

'"F"? repeated Nancy.

'That Ferrars fellow, I'll warrant,' continued Sir John, practically clapping himself on the back for such excellent guesswork. 'Here a week, he was. But hush,' he added. 'For it's a great secret!'

Elinor said nothing to confirm or deny his suggestion. Silence was the answer, she decided. Dignified silence.

If only Nancy had thought likewise. 'Edward Ferrars?' she repeated, pulling a face. 'That is to say, your brother-in-law, Edward Ferrars?'

'What about Edward Ferrars?' said Lucy, who had been attempting to engage Lady Middleton in conversation, to no avail, and now turned urgently to her sister.

'You know him?' asked Sir John.

'Oh, very well,' said Nancy.

'No, we don't,' snapped Lucy. 'Why ever would you say such a thing?'

'But you've met him?' ventured Elinor.

'Oh, only once or twice,' said Lucy vaguely. 'At my uncle's.'

During this strange exchange, Lucy's face had paled and was practically sickly. But, while Elinor very much wanted to know more about this uncle and the circumstances under which the Misses Steele had met Edward, she would have to wait several days for the terrible truth to come out.

CHAPTER NINETEEN

The day Lucy's secret finally spilled was a grey Wednesday, and while Marianne (who had not taken to either of the Misses Steele) preferred to stay at home with Mrs Dashwood and Margaret, Elinor had visited Barton Park, and agreed to allow Lucy to accompany her home.

'I hope you don't think I'm being nosy,' said Lucy. 'But I was wondering how well you knew Mrs Ferrars.'

Elinor did think she was nosy, but replied politely, if evasively. 'Not at all, really.'

'I hope you don't mind me asking,' said Lucy. 'Or think it strange.'

Elinor did mind and did think it was strange,

but again, chose to evade the suggestion. 'Have you met her?'

'Oh, no,' said Lucy, then went quiet for a moment. 'Such a shame you don't know her. I would so value your opinion.'

'My opinion?' repeated Elinor, losing her patience. 'I'm sure I don't know why. And I'm not sure I understand your interest, in any case.'

'No,' said Lucy. 'I'm sure you don't, given she is nothing to me at present. But, you see, she may be something to me soon. She may very well become . . . family.'

Lucy waited for the words to sink in.

'Family? You mean . . .' Elinor got it, or thought she did. 'You mean you're engaged to Robert Ferrars?' The idea of Lucy as a sister-in-law was not immediately pleasing.

'Robert?' replied Lucy. 'I never saw him in my life. No, it's with his younger brother I am . . . acquainted.' She eyed Elinor, awaiting a reaction.

Elinor, for her part, wobbled and had to stop
for a second to steady herself. 'You mean . . . that
is to say . . . you and Edward?' At the sound of his
name on her lips, she felt her heart contract.

'Yes. I know it must seem odd, for I've said
nothing – I even lied at dinner, when Nancy said
we knew him well. And I daresay he never
mentioned it to you when he was here.'

'No,' said Elinor curtly. 'He didn't.'

'It's a secret, you see. No one knows but Nancy,

and now you. Oh, you will keep it quiet, won't you?'

'I—'

'I shouldn't have said anything, I know,' said Lucy, knowing full well she had been determined to say as much as she could from the off. 'But you seem such a wise woman, and I do so want to know about Mrs Ferrars, and I don't think Edward will be cross as I know he looks upon you and Marianne as sisters.' Lucy smiled, as sickly sweet as syrup.

But Elinor barely noticed the dig. 'Sisters,' she repeated hazily. Then, coming to. 'How long have you and Edward—'

'Been engaged?' finished Lucy quickly and decisively. 'Four years.'

'Four?' Elinor could barely believe it. 'Well . . . congratulations.'

'Thank you,' simpered Lucy. 'He is wonderful, isn't he?'

Elinor nodded, for she could hardly argue with that.

'Though we're no closer to being wed now than when he proposed. And who knows how longer we may have to wait?' At that, Lucy took a miniature portrait from her pocket and showed it to Elinor. 'Poor man,' she said, gazing upon the picture of him. 'It does make him miserable.'

Elinor, looking at the likeness, remembered Edward's low spirits when he had arrived – no doubt straight from Lucy's company. After all, he'd said he'd been in Devonshire a while, hadn't he? She hadn't thought too long on it then, only been sad not to have had more time with him. But now she knew the awful truth.

'You won't tell, will you?' Lucy said again, as she snapped the miniature shut.

It took everything Elinor possessed to rally herself. But rally she did. 'No,' she replied. 'You can trust me.'

'Thank you,' replied Lucy. 'I wish I could say the same of Nancy. Not that she means badly, but she can't help blabbing.'

'I'm not a . . . blabberer,' said Elinor truthfully.

'I sometimes wonder if it's worth it,' said Lucy. 'All this secrecy, this painful separation. I sometimes wonder if I should end it, and his misery with it.'

Elinor would not allow herself to hope.

Quite right, for it was an absolute lie.

'Then I remember his proposal,' added Lucy slyly. 'The lock of hair I gave him.'

'Hair?' questioned Elinor.

'Oh, yes. He keeps it in a ring. I expect you saw it when he visited.'

Elinor, her stomach plummeting, nodded. Yes, she had seen it.

And she saw it again now in her mind: the brown curl in glass on a gold band. Of course it was Lucy's hair.

Not hers.

Lucy's.

CHAPTER TWENTY

Try as she might to imagine Lucy was lying, Elinor knew in her heart that this wasn't the case. Edward and Lucy were engaged. He had never loved her at all. He thought of her no more strongly than he thought of Marianne: as a sister.

What a fool she had been.

But then, what a fool Edward was to love Lucy, who was artless and ignorant, with an irritating sister! How could he be happy with her? If Mrs Ferrars disapproved of Elinor, she would surely loathe Lucy, whose connections were far less impressive.

Elinor's arrogance was out of character, though unsurprising. But even in her anger, she could not blame Edward for the mess. For had he promised her anything? Had he led her on? Made her believe he loved her when he didn't?

No, no and no. He had only enjoyed her company, as she had his. Very much.

But then again, he must surely have known of her affection for him – her sisters and mother certainly seemed to. So shouldn't he have left Norland as soon as he was aware of it? And never come to Barton at all? Oh, but if he had hurt her, he was the more injured one now, with only a life with Lucy to look forward to. And so, when she wept, as she did for several hours, Elinor found it was as much for Edward as for herself.

It was this belief in Edward's misfortune that helped Elinor keep her word to Lucy and breathe nothing of his secret engagement to her mother and Marianne, or, worse, Mrs Jennings. In fact, she found it almost a relief, as nothing they could have said would have made it any better, and had she told the truth, their disapproval of Edward would have been unbearable.

But as the days went on, and the wound began to scab, Elinor found herself with an overwhelming desire to pick at it. She wanted to know more about Edward and Lucy's arrangement and, with no one else to confide in or wheedle details from, she would just have to ask Lucy herself. Though that was proving harder than she had hoped.

Twice she had been to Barton Park since, but neither time had she been able to get Lucy alone for long enough, and so their exchanges were limited to what unseasonably nice weather they were having, and whether salmon was preferable to ham. But on the third occasion, Lady Middleton got her card table out. With Mrs Jennings, Sir John and Nancy engaged in a game of whist, and Marianne (who detested cards and had told everyone so) at the piano, Lucy was able to make some excuse about needing to finish her needlework, and Elinor, seeing her opportunity, said she would help her.

'So,' she began, once they were seated far enough in a corner to afford some privacy, 'tell me about Edward.'

CHAPTER TWENTY-ONE

Lucy, amused by Elinor's alleged affection towards Edward, (for he could hardly return it, not when he had such a prize in herself) was only too willing to divulge any and every titbit of information, having had to keep it to herself and Nancy until then.

'The situation with Edward is so difficult, you see,' she finished.

'I do see,' agreed Elinor, much as it pained her. 'Edward is dependent on his mother, I assume?'

Lucy nodded gravely. 'He has only two thousand pounds of his own and it would be madness to marry on that!'

'Madness,' repeated Elinor, thinking she might happily marry him for far less.

'Not that I'd mind making do,' declared Lucy. 'I'm used to it. But it wouldn't be fair on him to give everything up. No, we must wait, and wait for many years.'

Elinor checked herself. Perhaps she had been a little harsh on Lucy before. 'It must be hard.'

'Oh, yes!' said Lucy. 'But our bond is strong, don't you think?'

Elinor found, to her profound relief (for she had worried in her anger, that she was becoming a tad too like Marianne), that however much it saddened her, she did agree.

'He's never given me cause to doubt him,' continued Lucy. 'Never looked at another woman.'

Elinor quivered. 'Never?'

'No,' confirmed Lucy, her smile sly as a fox. 'Or I'd have known.'

'Of course,' said Elinor, shaking off her disappointment. 'So, what will you do now? Will Edward not risk upsetting his mother? It would surely only be for a while.'

'A while? We'll likely have to wait for her to die. Otherwise, she'll just give everything to Robert and be done with it.'

'You haven't met Robert?' checked Elinor, remembering.

Lucy shook her head. 'I hear he's a terrible show-off though.'

'A show-off?' came a screech, as a lull in the piano had allowed Nancy to catch the end of their conversation. 'Are you talking about your beaux again?'

'Don't be silly,' said Lucy. 'If we were, we'd hardly describe them as show-offs.'

'Well, Elinor's certainly isn't,' said Mrs Jennings, who fervently believed Sir John when he had guessed 'Ferrars', and agreed it was a handsome match. 'He's a modest and well-behaved sort. Though I couldn't tell you what Lucy's is like, she's so secretive.'

'I could. He's exactly as modest and well-behaved as Elinor's,' snapped Nancy, not realising how right she was.

Lucy bit her lip. Elinor reddened, in spite of herself. How little the others knew, for all their guesswork. Thankfully, Marianne chose that moment to begin a powerful and loud piano piece, so the two desperate ladies could whisper in secret once again.

'I do have one idea to fix it,' said Lucy. 'But I'll need your help.'

'I . . . of course.'

'I suppose you know Edward is keen on the church?' Lucy went on.

Elinor said she did.

'Well, would you . . . could you' – Lucy smiled sweetly – 'could you beg your brother John to find him a parish with a good living?'

Elinor frowned. 'But can't Edward ask? They are brothers-in-law, after all.'

'Well, he could,' admitted Lucy. 'But Fanny shares her mother's view on him joining the church.'

'Then I don't see how I can help.'

'Oh, it's impossible.' Lucy slumped at the seeming finality of it. 'Perhaps we should just end the engagement.'

Elinor hated herself for hoping and, besides, what did she have to hope for, for didn't Edward think of her as a sister?

'I said, perhaps we should end it,' repeated Lucy, not used to being ignored.

Elinor frowned. 'You're really asking me? But . . . whatever I say, you'll do what you want anyway.'

It was Lucy's turn to frown. 'No, I won't!' she insisted, but as she said it, she realised this was precisely the case and fell into silence, both women contemplating their fates as far as Edward Ferrars was concerned.

'When will you see him next?' asked Elinor eventually.

'January,' said Lucy. 'Nancy and I are going to London to stay with relatives. Will you be coming?' she added.

'Oh, no,' said Elinor quickly.

'That's a pity,' said Lucy.

Elinor nodded, suspecting Lucy meant quite the opposite, and for once, agreeing with her.

'But we have more than a month together until then!' said Lucy, painting on a smile. 'Won't that be nice?'

'Very,' said Elinor, doing the same.

But never had Elinor wished Christmas away so desperately, praying that January would arrive on the frosty doorstep and knock the very next morning.

CHAPTER TWENTY-TWO

January did come calling eventually, but it brought with it an offer that Elinor hadn't anticipated, and never imagined she would find herself saying yes to.

'London?' she asked.

'Just off Portman Square,' said Mrs Jennings. 'A handsome house – I go every winter – all the balls, you see. Such a wonderful season to spend in London. I'm sure your mother can spare you.'

'I . . .' The invitation had put Elinor on the spot, and Marianne's pleading looks were making it difficult to muster her usual excuses. To add to that, accommodation would be free, so their financial . . . *shortcomings* were no longer an issue.

'I won't take no for an answer,' said Mrs Jennings, adding to the inevitability.

'As long as Mama agrees,' said Elinor eventually. For she knew, however much being close to Edward might pain her, the chance of seeing Willoughby was doing quite the opposite for Marianne.

To Elinor's surprise and Marianne's delight, their mother did agree, and quickly. 'It will do you both the world of good,' she said. 'And Margaret too. She can concentrate on her lessons better with you two away.'

Margaret did not look at all as if this were welcome news, but no amount of pleading to go on her part would change her mother's mind on their separate fates.

'No, Margaret and I will be more than happy here. You two go and enjoy yourselves. And I daresay you'll be bumping into . . . old friends.'

Elinor knew exactly who her mother meant –
Edward – but couldn't tell her that her wishes
were pointless now, the match never even
possible, let alone the right one. And as for
Willoughby, Marianne had heard nothing from
him since the day he walked out of Barton leaving
her in tears and their match in apparent tatters, so
who knew what was going on there?

But, Elinor supposed, they might be about to
find out.

She only hoped it would have a happier ending
than her own.

CHAPTER TWENTY-THREE

The journey to London took three days. Three days in which Mrs Jennings barely stopped elaborating on all the things they may do in town, the people they may meet, the clothes they may buy. Three days in which Marianne smiled silently out of the window, leaving Elinor to answer their host's endless questions. Three days in which Marianne's anticipation swelled and Elinor's dulled to mere acceptance. Though perhaps, she told herself, this was all for the better. Willoughby was probably already in town, and so Marianne (and she and Mrs Jennings) would soon know, one way or another, what on earth was going on.

The house, Elinor had to admit when they finally arrived, was a fine one, and the sisters' rooms – Mrs Palmer's childhood apartment – were as elegant as their own back at Norland, though the view was rather more bustling and dusty.

'Oh, I love it!' declared Marianne, as she twirled across the carpet, evidently imagining the balls she would attend – no doubt on the arm of Willoughby. 'Dance with me, Elinor!'

Elinor, seated at the wide walnut desk, looked up. 'In a moment,' she said. 'I'm writing to Mama.'

An idea seized Marianne. 'Quite right!' she declared, and, taking a sheet of Elinor's paper and what must be Charlotte Palmer's old pen and ink, settled herself at a smaller bureau.

'Don't forget to ask after Margaret,' Elinor told her. 'The poor thing's quite put out at being "abandoned".'

'Oh, I'm not writing home,' explained Marianne.

'Then to whom?' asked Elinor.

But Marianne was mid-sentence and not to be disturbed, and then, the letter sealed, she rang for the footman and handed him the envelope in such a manner that Elinor could only guess

at the letter's destination: Willoughby, no doubt. A guess given further weight when, at dinner, Marianne could barely eat and then spent the evening with her ear at the window, listening for the clatter of carriage-wheels on cobbles. She had already been disappointed twice by knocks on the neighbour's door, when their own brass lion announced a visitor.

Marianne couldn't help herself. 'It's Willoughby!' she cried. 'I know it.'

But only moments later, her face fell as the man who entered the drawing room was not her supposed beau at all, but his greatest rival, Colonel Brandon. Marianne flounced out, leaving Elinor to welcome their guest.

'Is she ill?' asked the Colonel.

'Quite,' replied Elinor.

Although their conversation continued politely for almost an hour – with only one overexcited interruption from Mrs Jennings – Elinor found that she, too, was oddly disappointed at the identity of the guest. Though whether she wished it had been Willoughby for Marianne's sake, or someone else for her own, she refused to even guess.

But while Elinor's expectations lessened over the next few days, Marianne's only grew. Every morning she bounded out of bed to check for letters. Every knock at the door was greeted with bated breath and then a sigh and slump, if not a cross storming-off. At home, she could not concentrate long enough to play cards or even read. Out window shopping on Bond Street, it was evident to Elinor that her sister's eyes were not at all focused on hats or gloves or jewellery, but on

the passers-by, any one of whom may have been Willoughby, with his flashing eyes, his dashing demeanour.

And yet, as three weeks passed, and likely less than three miles between them, the man still managed to evade her.

It was almost as if he didn't wish to be found.

CHAPTER TWENTY-FOUR

Marianne was not one to imagine that Willoughby could be deliberately avoiding her, of course. No, instead she furnished her future husband with as many excuses as there were minutes in the day.

'What a glorious morning,' declared Mrs Jennings upon observing the sunshine warming the winter street below. 'Sir John won't want to abandon Barton for London if the weather is this fine. Oh, no. He'll be out hunting, mark my words.'

'Of course!' Marianne seized on that sentence as if it were gold. Willoughby must be hunting. That's why he hadn't come – he hadn't even read her letter yet.

As her sister hurried upstairs, Elinor could only suspect she was now writing to Somerset instead.

But as more days passed, there was still no sight or sound of him. And while Marianne spent many an hour at the window or door, testing the air for signs of frost or, better, snow, the only man to come calling – almost daily, in fact – was Colonel Brandon. Not that Marianne said more than a word to him, instead leaving Elinor to entertain him.

One afternoon, Colonel Brandon sat down to his cup of tea with an even graver face than usual.

'I hear . . .' he began, then checked himself. 'That is to say, I am told that your sister is definitely engaged now. To Willoughby,' he added, as if it were needed.

Elinor stiffened. 'And who told you?'

'Several people,' he said at last. 'Mrs Jennings for one. And . . . others.'

'You shouldn't listen to gossip,' said Elinor.

'I only wish to know if there is hope for me,' said the Colonel sadly. 'But I suppose not. No, all is lost.'

'But there's no evidence one way or another at the moment,' Elinor insisted.

The Colonel ignored her. 'Tell your sister I hope only for her happiness. And, when you see Willoughby, tell him I hope he deserves her.'

Elinor again tried to suggest that he lacked any proof of an actual engagement, but the Colonel would hear none of it, repeating his blustering wishes to the happy couple.

In fact, far from evidence of impending wedding bells, everything was pointing in a rather more grim direction. That very evening, Mrs Jennings brought news that Sir John, now residing in London himself, had bumped into Willoughby only hours before. Marianne's disappointment was clear to all. Elinor begged her to tell everything about what had passed that afternoon at Barton Cottage with Willoughby and begged her again to say if she was or wasn't actually engaged, but Marianne would say nothing on the subject at all.

So, she had no other choice, Elinor would have to write to her mother to demand that Mrs Dashwood ask her own daughter the same questions. For a child cannot lie to her parent, can she? Even if she may, perhaps, lie to herself.

It was only as she got into bed that evening that Elinor pondered Colonel Brandon's odd words: tell Willoughby I hope he deserves her.

Why wouldn't he deserve Marianne? Everyone had been so quick to praise him, after all. But then, Elinor recalled, what they had actually praised were his looks, his hunting skills, his ability to party.

Her stomach fell. Was Willoughby less of a gentleman than they had all supposed? Had he done something they didn't know about, other than seemingly disappear? Something terrible?

These, and several more pressing questions concerning Willoughby's intentions and reputation tormented Elinor as she fell into a fitful sleep.

She could not know that one of her queries, at least, would be answered the very next day.

CHAPTER TWENTY-FIVE

The invitation was hardly enticing: could Marianne and Elinor kindly accompany Lady Middleton to a party as Mrs Jennings was busy? But this was a party, and parties were Willoughby's territory, and so Marianne pleaded and Elinor conceded.

It began in the usual way: the carriage pulled up in its place in the queue, the ladies disembarked, were announced loudly to the crowd and said their hellos to the Lady of the House, whereupon they would be expected to spend the rest of the evening taking part in games of cards and polite conversation. But, while Lady Middleton immediately seated herself at the casino table, Marianne dragged Elinor to a prime spot from which they could scour the crowd for any sign of the elusive Willoughby. It did not take long to spot him.

'Oh, Elinor!' exclaimed Marianne. 'There he is!'

Elinor did not need to follow Marianne's gaze – she had already noticed him, and noticed too that, though he had clearly seen Marianne, he made no move towards her. Marianne waved frantically, and most indecorously, to no avail.

'Who is he talking to?' she demanded, referring

to a rather fashionable blonde. 'Why won't he come over?'

'Perhaps he hasn't seen you yet,' lied Elinor, trying to lower Marianne's flapping hands. 'And do try to calm down.'

But Marianne could not – or would not – calm down and soon Willoughby, along with a number of other guests, was forced to turn his head in Marianne's direction.

'Willoughby!' she cried, rushing towards him,

Elinor at her heels. 'At last!'

But if Marianne was hoping for a romantic reunion, she was to be at best disappointed, and at worst shocked. For it was to Elinor he addressed his questions as to the health of Mrs Dashwood and their enjoyment of London. He would not even meet his sweetheart's eye.

'What's going on?' Marianne demanded. 'Why won't you talk to me? Didn't you get my letters?'

'Yes,' he replied, finally, his eyes focused firmly somewhere over her shoulder. 'I got them.'

'Then why haven't you called on me? What's the matter? Have I done something wrong?'

But to these, and the volley of questions that followed, Willoughby said nothing more than 'goodbye', then bowed and rejoined his fashionable companion.

'Willoughby!' called Marianne.

But if she'd intended to follow him, Elinor's grasp on her arm prevented her. 'Help me,' she begged, her face paled to an almost ghost-like shade. 'There must have been some misunderstanding. I have to put it right!'

'Not now,' said Elinor sensibly.

'But I shan't be able to sleep until it's sorted,' wailed a far from sensible Marianne.

Thankfully, Willoughby chose that moment to leave the party altogether, and once Elinor had told Marianne this, the latter agreed, bitterly, to be taken home.

'What's wrong with her?' demanded a surprisingly wordy Lady Middleton as they clattered back to Berkeley Street.

'She just feels . . . a little unwell,' replied Elinor, as Marianne stared blankly from the carriage. 'I'm sure she'll recover in the morning.'

'I hope so,' said Lady Middleton, edging away.

Elinor hoped so too, with all her heart. But something inside told her that reality would be otherwise.

That something was right.

CHAPTER TWENTY-SIX

The letter arrived by afternoon post, in apparent reply to one Marianne had sent in desperation in her sleepless early hours.

My dear madam, it began.

I'm sorry you were offended by my behaviour last night. Though I cannot for the life of me work out what I did that was so very terrible. But still, if I have upset you, I apologise.

I also apologise if I ever gave you the impression you meant more to me than a friend. I thought I'd made it clear my affections were long-engaged elsewhere.

I'm returning your letters, as asked, as well as the lock of hair you foisted upon me.

I remain your most humble servant,

Willoughby

Humble? thought Elinor crossly as she reread the tear-stained and torn page. *Hardly.* Every line seemed written in villainy, every sharp full stop confirmation of his evil intent.

How could he lie like this? For it *was* all lies, she was sure of it. She'd seen his affections for herself, and they were most definitely directed towards Marianne. How could he? He was a damnable man!

Marianne's grief matched her sister's anger, and she wept as Elinor ranted, refused to eat and could not sleep. 'Oh, misery is me!' she wailed, as if it weren't obvious.

'You have to compose yourself,' insisted Elinor, trying to hold a spoonful of soup to her sister's lips. 'For Mama's sake.'

'I can't!' cried Marianne, batting the spoon away. 'My life is wretched. Don't you understand? I'm tortured!'

Elinor sought and found a crumb of comfort to offer instead. 'Isn't it better to have found out now what a scoundrel he is?' she said. 'Better than letting the engagement run on for months and months and have him jilt you at the altar?'

'Engagement?' said Marianne, her crying stopped in shock. 'We weren't engaged. Whatever gave you that idea?'

It was Elinor's turn to be stunned. 'But . . . he told you he loved you?'

Marianne squirmed a little. 'Not in so many words. I mean, he sort of implied it.'

Elinor's insides swilled suddenly, remembering Edward, and all that she had read – or misread – into his behaviour towards her. 'But you loved him,' she said. 'And he must have known so.'

Marianne nodded. 'I didn't foist the hair on him, you know,' she said then. 'He took it.'

Elinor snapped to. He *had* taken it! Her spirits lifted slightly: Willoughby and Edward were no more alike than she and Marianne. Elinor had mistaken Edward's affections; Marianne been deliberately misled.

'Poor Marianne,' she said kindly.

'Miserable Marianne!' raised her sister, and set to weeping again.

And so she would remain for many a day.

CHAPTER TWENTY-SEVEN

It was Mrs Jennings who eventually enlightened everyone as to where Willoughby's affections were otherwise engaged.

'Miss Grey?' repeated Elinor, placing her hand on Marianne's shaking shoulder. 'And you're sure this is true?'

'As true as the hair on my head!' exclaimed Mrs Jennings. 'I got it from Mrs Taylor, who got it from Mrs Higginthorpe, who got it from Miss Grey herself.'

'I don't understand,' said Elinor. 'Why?'

'Fifty thousand, she has,' said Mrs Jennings, as if she had laid the trump card. 'And by Mrs Taylor's accounts, he needs it. All that hunting and partying and carrying on about town.'

'She's rich, then,' said Elinor. 'Far richer than we.'

'But not half as handsome,' said Mrs Jennings. 'Not that that counts for a bean. I said, "Well, I hope she plagues his heart, the good-for-nothing scoundrel!"'

'Oh!' cried Marianne.

'There, there,' comforted Mrs Jennings. 'You mustn't upset yourself. There's plenty more men worth having – and worth having more than Willoughby.'

This information, however, only set Marianne off again and Mrs Jennings left with a sigh and a promise of sweetmeats at dinner. That would do it, she was sure of it.

But sweetmeats did not work, nor olives, nor the best place by the fire. In fact, none of Elinor's nor Mrs Jennings's indulgences could persuade

Marianne that there was still a drop of joy to be had in the world. In the end, she went to bed and so missed one of the most eligible of Mrs Jennings's 'plenty more men' call upon the house.

'Colonel Brandon,' Elinor said, as he entered the drawing room, bowed neatly and seated himself opposite her.

'Is it true?' he asked, his face almost contorted in pain.

'If by "it" you're referring to Marianne and Willoughby, then the sad answer is yes,' replied Elinor.

'The poor woman.' The Colonel shook his head.

'But where on earth did you hear it?' asked Elinor, suddenly aware that news like this wasn't conjured from nothing.

'In the stationer's on Pall Mall,' he replied. 'Oh, don't worry,' he added, seeing Elinor's aghast expression. 'Marianne wasn't mentioned. All talk was of Miss Grey's engagement.'

Elinor composed herself. 'And did they say when the wedding was scheduled?' *Oh, let it be soon*, she prayed silently. For the sooner he was wed, the sooner Marianne may heal and her mood may lift.

'Within weeks,' confirmed the Colonel.

Elinor nodded, brief relief sweeping over her.

'Tell me,' said the Colonel, leaning closer. 'Is your sister . . . is she in much pain?'

'Much,' said Elinor sadly. 'Though she weeps for nothing. You know they were never engaged?'

'What?' The Colonel shot upright.

'Not according to Willoughby or Marianne. Though I believe he deceived her into thinking they were.'

'But Marianne?'

Elinor shook her head. 'She still insists he is a good man at heart and it must be the world who has turned against her.'

'There she is quite wrong,' said the Colonel. 'Quite wrong indeed.'

Elinor smiled in sympathy. The Colonel may not be as openly passionate as her sister, but it was clear he felt as deeply and cared for her as much as Elinor herself.

She wasn't the only one to be pondering the thought.

'Two thousand a year,' said Mrs Jennings, after he'd gone. 'No debt or drawback other than the daughter. Though she can be farmed out to friends, I expect. And Delaford is monstrous pretty with all the conveniences. Lovely mulberry tree, a butcher's in the village and a nice spot to watch the carriages go by.'

'But—' began Elinor.

'No buts.' Mrs Jennings held up her hands. 'You mark my words: the Colonel and Marianne will be married by midsummer. All we need to do is put Willoughby out of her head.'

But that, Elinor suspected, would be easier said than done, even with Willoughby wed within weeks. For surely then he would return to his estate in Somerset, just miles from Barton Park. Meaning Marianne might never be rid of his memory or, worse, his wicked presence.

CHAPTER TWENTY-EIGHT

If Elinor had forgotten her plea to her mother to write to Marianne about Willoughby, Mrs Dashwood most definitely had not.

Mrs Jennings handed the letter to Marianne triumphantly over toast and marmalade one morning. 'Now, this must cheer you,' she announced. 'For what better solace than a mother's comfort?'

Of course, Mrs Dashwood offered no such thing, for the letter was full of Willoughby: how dashing he was, what a match they made, how she was sure the engagement must be official, so couldn't Marianne just let her know for sure, so she knew what to tell people?

Elinor paled with horror and guilt. 'I'll reply,' she said, laying her hand on her sister's arm.

Marianne shook it off. 'Just when I thought I might be feeling a little better, I am reminded of . . . him,' she wailed.

'You poor lamb,' said Mrs Jennings. 'Of course, what you need is a new beau. That would distract you. What better solace?'

'Please,' Elinor begged, gesturing for Mrs

Jennings to leave.

'Mark my words,' said Mrs Jennings slightly huffily, but left anyway as there was a hat on Duke Street that urgently needed buying.

'She doesn't even care,' snapped Marianne. 'She's only after gossip.'

'She's not,' replied Elinor, though knew Marianne was probably close to the truth.

Within seconds, there was another knock at the door.

'Am I never to be safe?' demanded Marianne. 'Perhaps we should go home. At least there I won't be tormented by gawpers and gossips.'

'It's only Colonel Brandon,' said Elinor, looking from the window to the street below. 'He won't gawp or gossip.'

But Marianne, doubting this as she doubted everyone now, took to her bed, leaving Elinor to entertain him once again.

'Tea?' she offered.

'No, I . . .' The Colonel seemed to be scrabbling for words or, perhaps, courage.

'What is it?' Elinor said, entreating him to sit down. 'You can tell me anything, you know?'

'I do know.' He nodded. 'You are a rock,' he added. 'For which I am grateful. But what I want— *need* to say isn't easy.'

'Is it Willoughby?' asked Elinor, her heart speeding in anticipation.

The Colonel seemed to brace himself. 'It is me,' he said. 'And, yes, Willoughby too. And a scandal, no less.'

And then he began the sorry tale.

CHAPTER TWENTY-NINE

Elinor could hardly believe what she was hearing. And yet, yes, it all made absolute sense.

The Colonel had talked first of his own lost love – a rich orphan raised as his sister, who was to be married against her will to his older brother in order to save the Brandons' crumbling fortune. Distraught, she and the Colonel – deeply in love – had tried to elope, but a maid betrayed them. The woman was returned to the Colonel's brother, and Colonel Brandon left for the East Indies with his regiment, believing it to be the best for everyone.

But when he returned, he discovered his cruel brother had divorced her, and she hadn't been seen since. Desperate, he said to Elinor, he had sought her high and low and found her, eventually, in a poorhouse, thin and pale and coughing blood.

'Consumption?' Elinor had asked.

The Colonel had nodded sadly and looked briefly to the window, as if for courage or comfort. Whichever – he found it, and continued. 'I placed her in care – the very best – but it was too late, she died within weeks.'

'So, where . . .' Elinor could not find the words.

'. . . does Willoughby fit in?' the Colonel finished for her.

Elinor nodded.

'The woman had a daughter called Eliza – neither mine nor my brother's, but a girl I loved as my own nonetheless.'

Elinor remembered Mrs Jennings's dollop of gossip before. But her version had been distorted, of course.

'I put her through school – boarding, of course, as I was away – then into the care of a woman in Dorset – not far from Barton Park – who had five other girls of a similar age. I was promised she would learn music and art, would be kept safe. And I thought she was.' He paused again. 'Until last November, when she disappeared.'

'Disappeared?'

'It turns out that music and art had been a little thin on the ground. In fact, she and the other girls had been out and about at all hours "gallivanting", I think the woman put it. With men.'

'Gallivanting,' repeated Elinor, an appalling image suddenly springing to mind of her own sister and Willoughby careening around the countryside in his carriage.

'For eight months I heard nothing, until a letter arrived when I was staying at Barton Park.'

'The day of the picnic!' said Elinor, as if she were a detective herself.

The Colonel nodded. 'She had had a child,' he said. 'The father, of course, had left her. In fact, had only stayed around long enough to take her . . . innocence before moving on to his next conquest.'

Realisation washed over Elinor like cold water. 'Willoughby,' she said.

'Yes,' said the Colonel. 'I'm afraid so.'

The Colonel's warning came back to her. 'That's what you meant when you said you hoped he deserved Marianne.'

'I'm sorry,' said the Colonel. 'I should have done more to stop them, or at least have told Marianne that Willoughby was disinherited.'

'Disinherited?' questioned Elinor.

'His aunt has left him penniless, by all accounts.'

'Oh!' she exclaimed.

'Quite,' replied the Colonel. 'That sort of scandal has a terrible effect on family relations.' He smiled, but thinly, for it was hardly a joke. Then, seized by conviction, added, 'But Marianne is better off now, do you see? And better off by far than my own Eliza.'

Elinor nodded.

'Though, of course, she is being taken care of now.'

'Of course,' she agreed.

Why, the contrast between the two men couldn't have been more evident. Perhaps this would be the golden ticket to make her sister see sense.

And not just about Willoughby, but about Colonel Brandon too.

CHAPTER THIRTY

If Elinor had been hoping for a sudden restoration in her sister's spirits, she was to be left disappointed. For, while Marianne agreed that Willoughby was indeed a scoundrel, she wept all the more at the truth about his poor character, wept for Eliza, then wept for herself again. Eventually she settled, but only into a kind of gloomy dejection.

Elinor's greatest wish – to return to Barton Cottage – was to be left unfulfilled as well. Her mother had written to say that not only was Marianne just as much at risk of 'enemy sightings' in Devonshire as in London, but also their stepbrother John was in town and the sisters should probably call on him and Fanny, if only out of duty.

While Marianne shrugged, not seeming to care any longer where she was, Elinor felt wretched. She had her own avoiding to be done, of course. She had no desire to spend a single second with Fanny, besides which, the chances of bumping into Edward if she were to call at her stepbrother's were high. But it was what her mother and Marianne wanted, and so, as she had done so many times before, she forced a smile and said it was an excellent idea.

And thus life in London continued.

Mrs Jennings spent a great deal of time damning Willoughby and claiming she knew he was a terror all along, while also managing to weasel the details of the wedding out of various acquaintances (the dress! The carriage! The hats!) and passing them on to Elinor.

And Colonel Brandon spent a great deal of time trying his best to cheer Marianne up. She had agreed to speak to him now, but it was only ever brief, much preferring to suffer in silence these days, forcing Mrs Jennings to recalculate her predictions for their own marriage from midsummer to Michaelmas.

And while Elinor did feel a sense of relief at Willoughby's wedding – the happy couple left the very same day for Somerset – it was to be short-lived, as the space he vacated was to be filled by several other unappealing prospects.

First, the Steele sisters turned up in town, eager to meet.

As if that wasn't bad enough, there was the matter of Fanny and John, and, though Elinor greatly wished it, they could not be avoided for ever.

CHAPTER THIRTY-ONE

In the end, fate chose who Elinor would meet and when.

She'd been on Bond Street selling some jewellery of her mother's, when she heard her name being called and turned, only to discover the voice belonged to none other than her stepbrother, John.

'How . . . lovely to see you,' she said.

'Likewise,' he replied. 'Of course, I would have called yesterday but Henry so wanted to see the wild animals at Exeter Exchange, and then we spent the rest of the day with Mrs Ferrars.'

Elinor flinched, but did not show it. 'How

thrilling that must have been,' she said, hoping that might be the end to the matter.

Of course it wasn't, as John demanded his sister accompany him on the walk back to his house.

'And Edward tells me you're settled at your little cottage,' he said as they walked. '"Charming" I think he called it. Fanny and I are so pleased.'

'I'm sure you are,' said Elinor stiffly.

'And I hear you're seeing a good deal of some chap called Brandon. Tell me, is he eligible?'

'Eligible?'

'His fortune,' explained John. 'How big is it?'

'Two thousand, I believe,' said Elinor, not sure what that had to do with her brother.

John frowned. 'Shame for you it's not double.'

'Why for me?' Elinor was baffled.

'Well, if you're going to marry him, I mean.'

'Marry him?' Elinor almost laughed. 'I don't think the Colonel has the slightest wish of marrying me.' Nor I him, she didn't bother to add.

'Well, no one's going to marry Marianne now, after . . . you know what.' He nudged her. 'And I'm sure you could persuade him. I know you're not rich, but you could make yourself' – he assessed her as if sizing up a horse – 'a bit prettier.'

Elinor reddened and found her fists clenching in irritation but said nothing.

'And we're all so eager to see you happy. Fanny and I, and Mrs Ferrars, too.'

Elinor flinched this time. 'Mrs Ferrars?'

'Oh, yes, she said as much the other day.'

What business could it be of hers? Elinor wondered, then remembered with a horrible jolt the woman's wishes to keep 'unsuitable' women away from her sons. Another shock was to follow.

'It would be rather wonderful to have my sister and Fanny's brother marry at the same time.'

Elinor frowned in renewed confusion. 'Robert is going to be married?'

'Oh, not Robert,' said John with a smile. 'Edward!'

It took a moment for Elinor to restore herself to something resembling calm. 'To whom?' she managed at last.

'The Honourable Miss Morton. Thirty thousand she has.'

Miss Morton? But what of Lucy? Elinor could

hardly believe this.

'And Mrs Ferrars will give him a thousand a year once it's settled,' John carried on.

'So it's not settled yet?' Elinor practically snatched at the faint ray of hope.

'Not yet,' admitted John. 'But Mrs Ferrars is bound to have her way. Such a determined woman. And generous too. Why, only last week she pushed two hundred pounds into Fanny's hands. Good job too, given all the expenses at Norland.'

'Expenses?' said Elinor, barely listening now.

'Well, there's all the linen and china we had to replace,' he said, pointedly. 'And I had to buy a farm.'

'You "had" to?'

'Absolutely. It would have been foolish not to. And Fanny has her heart set on a greenhouse.'

'Naturally,' said Elinor, with just a hint of bitterness in her words, like a drip of lemon on sugar.

'Ah, here we are,' said John as they arrived at Conduit Street. 'Well, it's been a pleasure. I can hardly wait to tell Fanny I saw you. She and Mrs Ferrars were most concerned that you were keeping company with . . . unsavoury types. Mrs Jennings,' he added. 'I suppose you know her husband got his money in a . . . low way.'

'By working?' suggested Elinor, with more than a touch of sarcasm.

'Well, yes!' said John. 'But you seem perfectly . . . respectable still. I'm sure Fanny will be relieved. As will Mrs Ferrars.'

'Lucky me,' said Elinor.

But she had never felt quite as unlucky in her life.

What Elinor had been desperate to ask her brother, but could not, of course, was whether Edward was in town. In the end, Edward confirmed it himself, calling no less than twice in two days at Mrs

Jennings's house. This pleased Elinor immensely, almost as much as the fact she'd been out both times. But she couldn't avoid him for ever. Not least as she and Marianne had been invited to dinner at Fanny and John's, along with the Middletons, the Misses Steele and, of course, Mrs Ferrars. And if Mrs Ferrars were there, then – perish the thought! – Edward may well be too. But even if he were, then meeting the dreaded Mrs Ferrars would at least be interesting, now that Elinor had nothing to lose. Though she wasn't sure Lucy would be so blasé. Did the poor girl even know about the Honourable Miss Morton and Mrs Ferrars's intentions for her son's marriage?

Well, they would find out tonight, surely. Because if there was one thing parties were never short on, it was drama.

CHAPTER THIRTY-TWO

'Pity me!' said Lucy, as they walked up the stairs together. 'Nobody here but you knows what torment I'm going through!'

'I feel your pain,' said Elinor truthfully, as, despite being told Edward was not attending, she found herself to be a bundle of nerves.

Though Lucy was far more interested in someone else. 'In a moment,' she continued. 'I will meet the woman who will become my mother-in-law!'

And there it was: the poor girl had no clue about Miss Morton. And though she could have put her out of her misery with the truth, instead

Elinor did indeed choose to pity her. (A fact that probably irritated Lucy, who preferred to be envied, whatever she might imply.) For, whoever's mother-in-law she was destined to be, nothing could change the fact

that Mrs Ferrars was a devil of a woman. Thin, stiff and small, much like her daughter, she was serious to the point of sourness and sallow on top of it, so that the overall effect was of an unripe lemon.

In short, Elinor did not like her. And, not that it mattered any more, Mrs Ferrars clearly did not like Elinor back. But what was odd (and would have been funny if it hadn't been so tragic) was that the woman seemed completely charmed by the Misses Steele: Nancy was allowed to blab freely about her latest beau – a doctor of some sort – while Lucy found herself the object of much attention, a fact she foolishly took to be evidence of Mrs Ferrars' approval, smiling smugly at all times.

At least the dinner was bearable and showed no signs of John's claimed financial worries: the food was lavish, the servants numerous and the wine flowing as freely as water. If only the same could be said of the conversation.

'Oh, but Henry is much taller than William,' insisted Fanny, comparing her own son to one of Lady Middleton's. 'Don't you agree, Lucy?'

'I . . . well, that is to say, I'm not sure,' said Lucy, torn between pleasing her future mother-in-law and her own cousin, Mrs Jennings.

'I think they're both the tallest,' said Nancy stupidly.

Elinor winced. 'William's got at least an inch on Henry,' she declared, earning herself glares from both Fanny and Mrs Ferrars.

Marianne rolled her eyes. 'Does it matter?' she demanded. 'Can't we talk about . . . music, or – or art!'

'If you wish,' said Mrs Ferrars thinly.

'Then what of those sketches?' Marianne suggested, nodding at two framed pieces on the wall. 'Those are Elinor's, aren't they?'

Elinor blushed as everyone turned to her, for they were hers indeed: presents for her brother, before . . . everything.

Mrs Ferrars squinted. 'They're competent,' she conceded.

'Though hardly a patch on Miss Morton's,' added Fanny.

Elinor flinched.

Marianne frowned. 'What's this Miss Morton got to do with anything? Who is she, anyway?'

Mrs Ferrars smiled unpleasantly. 'She's Lord Morton's daughter, of course.'

'Excellent at everything,' added Fanny, then turned pointedly to Elinor. 'And pretty with it.'

Elinor said nothing. Then or later. But she knew full well what had been implied: that Miss Morton was a catch. And she, decidedly, was not.

The only consolation was that Lucy would be lumped in with Elinor as unsuitable. If, of course, Mrs Ferrars had known the truth about the secret engagement. But she was as blind to it as Lucy was to the 'alternative arrangements' Mrs Ferrars had in mind.

CHAPTER THIRTY-THREE

'I can't believe I ever dreaded meeting Mrs Ferrars!' Lucy blurted to Elinor the next morning. 'She obviously adores me. Did you see how she flattered me?'

'She was certainly . . . civil,' said Elinor, not wishing to encourage anything.

'Oh, but she was more than that!' insisted Lucy. 'She liked me best of everyone there, it was as plain as the nose on your face.'

Elinor, who had always had high regard for her own nose, petite as it was, was tiring quickly of this issue. 'If she'd known about you and Edward, then, yes, this would all be wonderful news, but the fact is, she doesn't.'

'Well, you *would* say that,' said Lucy, crossing her arms. 'She likes me, and so does Fanny, and that is all that matters.'

Elinor knew it was less than a fraction of what mattered, given the truth, but said nothing.

Lucy went on. 'And now I'm in with Fanny, I daresay I shall be spending most of my time there, and Edward is bound to show up at some point. Won't that be wonderful?'

Elinor's stomach jumped at the thought, and it took all she had to muster a smile. 'Quite.'

But the relief Elinor felt that she, at least, would not be party to this was brief, as the footman chose that very moment to enter and announce that she had a guest.

'Oh, who can it be?' asked Lucy, still basking in her own delight. 'Your own beau?'

'Mr Ferrars,' replied the butler.

'Robert?' asked Lucy, intrigued. 'Oh, you dark horse, Elinor.'

'Not Robert,' corrected the footman. 'The man said his name was Edward.'

If Lucy was surprised, then Edward was more so when he entered the room to find both women standing there.

'I . . . well, how nice,' he said, looking as if he wanted to back out of the room quicker than he had come in.

'Edward,' said Elinor awkwardly.

Lucy merely nodded – of course Edward didn't know that Elinor knew about the secret engagement, so an air of mystery must be kept up.

The air was as thick and sliceable as butter.

'Do sit down,' said Elinor eventually, remembering her manners. This was all absolutely fine, she told herself. Edward would soon be gone. There was no reason to be jittery.

If only Marianne had thought the same. 'Edward!' she cried, rushing into the room.

'I thought I heard you. Oh, how good it is to see you. Isn't it good, Elinor?' she entreated her sister.

Elinor met Edward's gaze briefly, then quickly looked at her shoes. 'Of course,' she replied. 'The Ferrars are always welcome.'

'Except Fanny,' said Marianne, without thinking.

'Marianne!' scolded Elinor.

'Sorry. I forget she's your sister,' explained Marianne to Edward. 'You're so . . . different.'

'She is sharp and I dull, you mean,' said Edward. 'Isn't that what you thought?'

Marianne, remembering her earlier dismissal of him, blushed. 'If I gave you that impression, then I apologise. I couldn't be happier to see you. And not just for Elinor's sake.'

At that, Edward and Elinor met eyes again briefly, unseen by Lucy, who was stuck in a corner being ignored, a state of affairs she was not accustomed to.

'I'm glad you stayed in London,' said Edward, and, though his eyes were on Marianne, Elinor felt sure the words were directed at her. But why? What was happening?

'Not for long,' said Marianne. 'We're back to Barton soon. In fact—' She clapped her hands in delight as an idea popped into her head. 'You should accompany us! Shouldn't he, Elinor?'

Elinor said nothing.

Edward only mumbled.

'Anyway, why weren't you at dinner yesterday?' demanded Marianne, asking the question on both women's lips.

'I . . . I was otherwise engaged.'

Marianne frowned. 'But surely it was more important to see us?'

Whatever cat had hold of Lucy's tongue before, suddenly let go. 'Perhaps you think all men break their *engagements*,' she snapped in Marianne's direction.

At that Elinor felt her chest tighten, though, incredibly, Marianne continued, oblivious. 'Oh, not at all. I know Edward to be the most honest and kind of men. Elinor has always said so.'

Edward stood, suddenly flustered. 'I think I must be going,' he said.

'Already?' asked Marianne.

Lucy rose quickly. 'Me too,' she said, then turned to Edward. 'Perhaps, as you are so *kind*, you can walk me.'

'I . . . of course,' he replied, and with a brief bow, followed Lucy through the door.

The room seemed to heave in relief at their departure.

'That wretched woman,' said Marianne. 'What was she playing at, hogging Edward like that when she could see he wanted to talk to you? She barely even knows him.'

'Lucy's known him longer than any of us,' said Elinor, ever the diplomat. 'She's perfectly entitled.'

'Oh, for heaven's sake,' snapped Marianne. 'How can you be so . . . forgiving all the time?'

'Because I have to be,' said Elinor eventually.

Because it was that or let jealousy eat her up as if she were a sweetmeat herself.

CHAPTER THIRTY-FOUR

London being London, several events occurred before the Dashwood sisters could even begin to think of packing to return to Devonshire.

Firstly, Mrs Palmer had her baby, meaning Mrs Jennings was often out of the house, attending to her new grandson, dear little Thomas.

Next, Elinor met Mr Robert Ferrars, and decided he was indeed a fool and a show-off, and wondered how on earth Edward was related to such a boor.

Thirdly, and most significantly, Fanny invited the Misses Steele to stay. This, for Elinor, was an end to the notion that Edward had any affection for her, still less that she stood a chance of ever becoming a Ferrars herself. For surely this was a sign that Mrs Ferrars had changed her mind about the Honourable Miss Morton and was ready to welcome Lucy into the family.

Signs, however, have a tendency to be misread, especially by lovelorn young ladies. And in this case, both Lucy and Elinor had misjudged the situation terribly.

It was Mrs Jennings (who else?) who brought the news.

'You won't believe it!' she announced, bustling in with a red face and the residue of baby sick on her shoulder.

'Believe what?' asked Elinor, barely looking up from her cup of tea. This sort of disturbance was a frequent occurrence with Mrs Jennings and the gossip often turned out to be less than thrilling, even if it was true.

'Remember that gentleman?' Mrs Jennings

heaved herself into a seat, fanning herself despite the winter chill.

'What gentleman?' asked Elinor, hoping to heaven it wasn't news of Willoughby that might revive Marianne's moping.

'The "F" fellow. Ferrars!' said Mrs Jennings, as if she should have known, adding, 'Edward,' before Elinor could ask which one.

Elinor paled. 'Yes. I—'

'I used to think you and he had something but Lord, I'm glad I was wrong.'

Now, Elinor went from ghost to tomato. 'What on earth—'

'He's only been engaged for twelve months. *Twelve months!* Can you believe it? And who to, you might ask? Well, only to one Lucy Steele. My own flesh and blood and she didn't even hint at it. No one knew, apart from that sister of hers, Nancy, and Lord only knows how she kept it in for so long, the mouth she has on her.'

Elinor said nothing, not a word of correction or inquisition. She didn't need to, as Mrs Jennings was still in full flow.

'Of course, it was that Nancy who let the cat out of the bag in the end. Blabbed it to Fanny, who had quite the hysterics, by all accounts. Turns out Lucy wasn't in Mrs Ferrars's sights at all, least not as a daughter-in-law. Anyway, she sent the Misses Steele packing that very minute. Barely gave them time to find their suitcases.'

'And Edward?' asked Elinor, taking advantage of Mrs Jennings's need to take a breath.

'Oh, I daresay he'll be all of a tither when he finds out. Though if he does love her – and I don't doubt he does – then I'm quite sure he'll marry her regardless of his mother's opinion. Why shouldn't he? She's a fine girl. Fine girl. None better. And even if Mrs Ferrars only gives him five hundred a year, they'll cope. I can always help out. Find them a housemaid, perhaps.'

At this thought, Mrs Jennings hurried out again, perhaps to secure that very housemaid, leaving Elinor to the cold comfort that at least now she was no longer carrying around such a secret. At least now, she could admit the truth to her sister.

'And when did you find out?' asked Marianne. 'Just this minute?'

Elinor had no need to lie any longer. 'Four months ago,' she admitted.

'Four *months*?'

Elinor nodded. 'And it's four years they've been engaged. Not a year.'

Marianne let out a cry. 'Oh, Elinor! Why didn't you say something?'

'I wanted to,' she said. 'But that would have broken my promise to Lucy.'

'And all the while you tended to my broken heart, your own was breaking!' Marianne looked close to fainting with the weight of it.

'I'm quite all right,' assured Elinor. 'Really. I wish them both happiness.'

'But what about your happiness?'

'Mine?' asked Elinor. 'I'm not sure I believe it can be gained from a constant attachment. Not any more. And that is perfectly fine. Really, it is,' she added, seeing Marianne was about to argue.

And so she told herself for the rest of the day. By the time she finally climbed into bed and snuffed out the light, she almost believed it.

CHAPTER THIRTY-FIVE

If Elinor hoped the matter was over, now the truth about Edward was out, she was to be sorely disappointed, for the morning brought a visit from her brother, with news that poor Fanny was still reeling at the proceedings.

'Shocked, she was,' he exclaimed. 'Quite, quite hysterical and rightly so. The doctor says it's lucky she has such a strong character, or her heart could have stopped. As it is, she's taken to her bed and says she can never think kindly of anyone ever again after such a deceit.'

Elinor was surprised to hear she'd ever thought kindly in the first place, but merely painted her face with concern.

'Of course, Mrs Ferrars was even more horrified,' John went on. 'She'd been planning a most eligible connection for him, and all the time Edward had been sneaking around like a fox. A fox, I tell you! Already engaged to someone so utterly unsuitable it never entered anyone's head to make the match. Well, Mrs Ferrars has given him a piece of her mind now.'

'She has?' In spite of herself, Elinor felt her pulse quicken.

John nodded. 'Not that Edward was having any of it. Not when she offered him the Honourable Miss Morton. Not when she threw in the Norfolk estate. Not even when she said she'd cut him off without a penny if he persisted in his wishes. Of course, it's Robert who's laughing. He'll end up with the lot.'

'So that's it?' demanded Marianne. 'Edward gets nothing?'

'Oh, his two thousand will remain his. But his mother says she's done with him. And if he tries to get a proper job, she'll put a stop to that too.'

'But she can't!' protested Elinor, indignant now. 'That's . . . heartless.'

John frowned. 'It's no more than he deserves. And she can do as she likes, and will, too.'

Elinor bit her tongue on her bitter reply and asked instead as to Edward's whereabouts.

'In a tavern, I suppose. He'll have to find his own lodgings, of course. Though it's Lucy I feel sorry for. Not much of a prospect now, is he? Not even for someone like her.'

Neither sister took the bait on that, for both knew they were markedly lower in John's rankings than even Lucy. Instead, Marianne wished their sister-in-law well in her recovery, and Elinor bade John goodbye, claiming prior engagements of her own.

Of course, she had none. Only to return to the house to endure the endless gossip that was handed over the Bond Street shop counters like small change and then passed into the pocket of Mrs Jennings and thence to Elinor: that they'd been engaged for a decade; that there was a secret love-child squirrelled away in Somerset somewhere; that Edward had broken his engagement to Lucy after all. Thankfully Elinor knew all to be concoctions, as frothy and ephemeral as lace trimming.

It was two days before any further facts were handed her way, and even these may have been exaggerated, coming as they did from Nancy Steele.

'He's talking about joining the church again,' she told Elinor. 'But he'll have to be a vicar and how can they live on that sort of money? If he can even find a village in need of one. Of course, they'll want me to go begging to my friend to ask if he can help. Can you imagine? I'll do no such thing.'

But it was not to Nancy the pair went begging. Instead, a letter came the next morning addressed to Elinor, asking her again if she might put in a good word to Sir John or Mrs Jennings, who might in turn put in a good word where a place with a decent living might be available. Because until he found one, they might never get married.

Elinor quickly fulfilled her responsibility by handing the letter over to Mrs Jennings, who received the news of her vast influence with delight and set about to find Edward a position as a vicar as well as the housemaid already on her list.

CHAPTER THIRTY-SIX

In the end Mrs Jennings did find Edward a position, though rather by accident than intention. She'd been offering gossip to Colonel Brandon along with his tea and happened to mention that poor Edward and Lucy couldn't marry until he had a job, only none could be found.

Two days later, the Colonel called again, this time for Elinor expressly.

'I have heard,' he said, 'that your friend Mr Ferrars has been dealt a dastardly hand by his own mother, just for persevering with a deserving woman.'

Elinor was not sure she would have put it quite like that, but nodded anyway.

'Such cruelty,' continued the Colonel, 'to divide young lovers like that. I know only too well what they each might be driven to . . .'

Elinor remembered his story and put a hand to her mouth. 'Of course,' she said.

'Well, I would like to help him, if I might. You see, the parsonage in my own parish at Delaford is vacant. The living's not worth a lot – no more than two hundred a year – but it's his if he would like it.'

'Oh, Colonel,' said Elinor, as touched as she was astonished. 'That is kind.'

'It's nothing, really.'

'But it is,' she said. 'You are a good man. He and Lucy will be grateful, I am sure.'

'Lucy,' he repeated. 'Oh, I'm not sure she will. Two hundred won't be enough to support her, let alone a family. The wedding is still some way off, I imagine.'

'Nevertheless,' said Elinor, pretending she felt nothing at that prospect. 'It is incredibly generous.'

Such was the smile Colonel Brandon gave Elinor, and she him, that Mrs Jennings might have been forgiven for mistaking their happiness for something else entirely as she peered in through the drawing room window.

For mistake it she did.

★★★

'Oh, I wish you all the joy in the world!' she declared, bursting in the moment the Colonel was gone.

Elinor frowned. 'Well, it is a matter of joy,' she admitted. 'Colonel Brandon is one of a kind. Though I am surprised at it, really. I didn't think he would be quite so compassionate.'

'Oh, you do yourself down,' said Mrs Jennings. 'I never doubted it.'

'But don't tell a soul. Not even Lucy,' begged Elinor. 'I will write to Edward myself.'

Mrs Jennings frowned. 'Really? Edward?'

'Well, yes. He'll have to be ordained soon.'

'Will he?' Mrs Jennings was struggling now. *Unless . . . he would be the one to marry them himself. That must be it!* 'Oh, I understand. Very nice too.'

And, pleased as punch, the woman bustled out to pass on the good news to Sir John (for surely he didn't count as 'a soul') when who should she bump into but Edward. 'Oh, the very man himself!' she declared. 'Such wonderful news Elinor has for you!'

Baffled, Edward entered the drawing room. But his confusion ended swiftly, as Elinor did indeed pass on wonderful news.

'The Colonel?' he said again in happy astonishment. 'I must thank him myself.' And he stood, only having sat down two minutes before.

Though she had completely forgotten to ask what he had come for, Elinor was not sorry to see him go. In fact, Edward's arrival had quite discombobulated her, given that she hadn't set eyes on him since before the engagement was . . . made public. And now, she would not see him again until he was Lucy's husband. Very possibly thanks to her intervention. The irony did not escape her.

But if she had thought to ponder on this longer, she wasn't given the chance to, as in burst Mrs Jennings again, eager to hear what Edward had thought of the Colonel's 'offer' and how soon he might be ordained in order to do the deed.

'A few months?' she screeched when Elinor told her. 'And is the Colonel happy to wait that long?'

'I'm not sure the Colonel minds one way or another.'

'Minds if he doesn't marry you? I should say he'd mind.'

Elinor frowned. And then laughed. 'Oh, Mrs Jennings, you thought *I* was to marry *Colonel Brandon*?'

'Why, yes. Aren't you?'

'Oh, no,' said Elinor. 'No one is marrying anyone. Not yet.' And she explained what the Colonel had really come for.

'Oh, well, he's wrong if he thinks Lucy and Edward won't wed yet. You mark my words, they'll be down the aisle at Delaford before Michaelmas.'

So, Elinor marked them, for had Mrs Jennings's words been wrong yet?

CHAPTER THIRTY-SEVEN

The latest turn of events had convinced Elinor and Marianne that the time had come to leave the bustle of London and return to the relative calm of Barton Cottage. The journey, though, was a long one and, despite her sister's slight revival, Elinor was not convinced Marianne could do it in one go. Instead she suggested taking up the Palmers' offer to stop off at Cleveland, their estate in the country. A suggestion that was not met kindly.

'Cleveland?' demanded Marianne. 'Absolutely not.'

'But, Marianne, you don't understand—'

'No, it's you who doesn't understand. Cleveland is in Somerset and I cannot go to Somerset under any circumstances. Not after—' At this she broke off, obviously tormented by the thought of Willoughby, and the new Mrs Willoughby, settled in Combe Park in marital bliss.

Elinor tried another tack. 'But Mama is so desperate to see you, and this is the only way, really it is.'

'Desperate?' asked Marianne wanly.

'Desperate,' confirmed Elinor. 'Really, we won't stop for long and Barton is but a day from Cleveland.'

'And then we'll be home,' realised Marianne.

'And then we'll be home,' repeated Elinor, peace filtering through her at the very thought.

Marianne thus convinced, in early April, the sisters said their fond farewells to the Middletons, and less fond ones to Fanny and John. Accompanied by Mrs Jennings, they set off along filthy streets for the clean air of country, and Somerset.

★ ★ ★

Cleveland was a handsome estate indeed. The gardens were extensive, and the sweep of the gravel drive was lined with Lombardy poplars, tall and proud and straight as soldiers. So handsome, in fact, that they had barely descended from the carriage when Marianne begged to get out.

'But we can walk the grounds later. Don't you want to see the house?' asked Mrs Palmer. 'The china is quite something! And the carpets. Marvellous, aren't they, dear?' She turned to Mr Palmer.

'No,' he replied, as irritable as ever.

'I'm sure Elinor would love to see them,' replied Marianne. 'But it's been months since I was in the country and I do so love the grass, the trees, the view! Why, I'm sure I can see Barton from here if I try!'

Marianne seemed so enthused – more than she had been since the whole Willoughby hoo-ha – that in the end Elinor let her go. Perhaps, she hoped, her sister was over the worst after all.

If only she'd followed her, she would have found the girl on top of the hill behind the house scanning the horizon not for Barton Park, but for Willoughby's own estate at Combe.

The next morning, Marianne announced she was

to take to the hills again. But, when she looked from the window, a battalion of black clouds forced her sister into action.

'It's impossible,' Elinor insisted. 'You don't want a . . . repeat of last time.' The image of a soaking wet Willoughby, the injured Marianne over his shoulder, sprung uncomfortably to mind. And Elinor suspected Marianne was imagining the very same.

'But I'll only be an hour or so,' she pleaded, 'and the clouds are practically at Combe— I mean Barton!'

Elinor knew it. 'But—'

'I wish you'd stop fussing. I'll be perfectly fine.'

Fine she was for the first thirty minutes, until the clouds – which, she admitted, had perhaps only been a few miles away after all – decided to unload their burden all over Marianne.

'Oh, bother,' she declared as she hurried back to the grounds, slipping on the spring grass.

This time, she managed to stay upright, but everything about her was sodden, a fact that didn't escape the gentleman visitor who had spotted her as he arrived on the drive.

'Marianne?' he called.

Marianne looked up, having been concentrating firmly on her feet. If she was disappointed, she didn't show it. 'Colonel Brandon!'

'Allow me,' he said, offering his arm (well, wet socks hardly warranted Marianne being thrown over his shoulder).

Incredibly, Marianne did as he asked. She changed out of her wet clothes at his suggestion. She sat next to him at dinner. And, when he expressed concern over dessert that she might be getting a cold, she went to bed on his recommendation.

'I'll be fine by the morning,' she insisted. 'You'll see. Quite fine!'

CHAPTER THIRTY-EIGHT

Marianne, being Marianne, and prone to tragedy of all sorts, was, of course, far from fine.

Though she was determined to get up to prove her strength, she then sat shivering by the fire, her face pale as milk and her nose scarlet from all the sneezing.

'You're feverish,' said Elinor, her cool hand on her sister's hot forehead.

'Nonsense,' said Marianne, batting it away feebly. 'It's just heat from the flames.'

But by lunch, unable to muster the energy to cut up her gammon, let alone swallow any of it, she let herself be persuaded back to bed.

'Here,' said the Colonel, bending to lift her (well, this was a different situation – not just wet socks, any more).

'Don't be silly,' said Marianne, though without real conviction. 'You can't possibly.'

But he could and he did.

'I'll be fine by the morning,' she said again, her arms around his surprisingly sturdy shoulder. 'We can still go home tomorrow.'

'Of course you can,' said the Colonel, and carried on up the stairs.

But the next morning, poor Marianne couldn't

even sit up and the doctor was ordered as a matter of urgency.

To the Colonel's relief, the doctor, a sallow man with a face like a gravestone, said he was sure she would live. However, he did mention the words 'putrid' and 'infection', which were enough to send Mrs Palmer scuttling off to Bath with the baby, lest it should catch something, and Mrs Jennings off to the village to tell anyone who might listen.

Elinor, meanwhile, sat next to her sister's bed and despaired. Marianne was so weak from her previous trials that Elinor believed it might be weeks before they saw their mother again.

If at all.

No, no, she must put that awful thought out of her mind. The doctor said she would live, and he was a qualified man, and knew about these things. Still, it was a worry.

The only person more concerned than Elinor was

Colonel Brandon, who checked on the patient almost hourly, and spent several evenings reading to her from her novels. And though she only opened her eyes on occasion, he felt sure she appreciated it.

Elinor certainly did, convinced that he was twice the man Willoughby had been, if only Marianne would get well enough to see it. But still the patient showed little sign of improvement. 'Can I see Mama?' were her only words. And always Elinor had to disappoint her, for Barton remained a day away, however much they both wished it closer.

But when Marianne repeated her wish for the umpteenth time that day, Elinor had an idea: perhaps she would write to their mother and beg her to come. The sight of her may restore Marianne, after all. Yes – she snatched at something tangible to do – she would write this minute!

But, when, letter in hand, she sought out the

Colonel to post it for her, he had an even better idea. 'I will fetch her myself,' he said.

'Really?' said Elinor. 'You don't have to, I'm sure a servant . . .'

But the Colonel was already buttoning his coat and setting off to summon his carriage.

CHAPTER THIRTY-NINE

By the following evening, Elinor's spirit had been restored: not only were Mrs Dashwood and the Colonel expected back any minute, a visit from the lofty doctor had confirmed an improvement in her sister.

'A vast one,' he declared. 'Quite a recovery. I thought she was a goner, but there you go.'

And so it was with clear eyes and a full heart that Elinor awaited the sound of carriage wheels on gravel, and threw open the door herself when, at ten, the knock finally came.

But at the sight of the caller, her joy, her strength, her words all departed like scattering crows. For there, on the doorstep, stood none other than Willoughby, looking dishevelled and decidedly desperate.

'What on earth?' Elinor managed, as he walked boldly into the hall, dripping water all over the marvellous carpet.

'I came as soon as I heard,' he said.

'Heard what?'

'That Marianne was ill. "Putrid" in fact. Can it be true?'

That wretched Mrs Jennings, thought Elinor grimly. 'No, it isn't. She's getting better every hour. Though I don't know what business it is of yours.'

Willoughby seemed to reel in relief. 'Thank heaven. I thought . . . I thought I might be too late.'

'For what? To break her heart all over again?'

The man wobbled and steadied himself on a banister. 'No, I—'

'Willoughby, have you been drinking?'

'A bit,' he admitted. 'But for Dutch courage only. You see, I came to beg forgiveness.'

Elinor steadied herself, though it was anger that rattled her rather than alcohol. 'Well, you can go again. She forgave you months ago. More's the pity.'

'Really? Without knowing the truth?'

'What truth?' demanded Elinor. 'That you were gallivanting around with other women?'

'No. Well, yes. But what matters is why. You see I have never been rich, but my tastes are expensive.'

Elinor sighed, feeling she was in for a long and sorry tale. 'You may as well sit down.'

Elinor was right, the tale was indeed a long and sorry one: mounting debts, his ailing aunt who would not hurry up and die, the importance of marrying a woman with a vast fortune.

'So, you see your sister was entirely unsuitable.'

'I see,' said Elinor, her voice as bitter as lemon.

'But you don't!' declared Willoughby. 'The thing is, I knew she was the wrong one for me, but I couldn't help myself. I fell in love with her anyway.'

Elinor frowned. 'Not enough to stop you marrying Miss Grey, though.'

'No,' he admitted, with the sulk of a small boy deprived of his favourite toy. 'And now I'm doomed to misery because of it.'

'Poor you,' said Elinor. 'Frankly, your attempts to explain yourself away are pathetic. And anyway, what about Eliza?'

At that name, Willoughby baulked. Though not for long. 'Well, she was so insistent. Followed me around like a dog.'

'Oh, so it's her fault?'

'Just because I'm a swine, doesn't make her a saint. Anyway, I could hardly have married *her*.'

'Why are you here?' Elinor said then. 'Really?'

Willoughby slumped. 'I miss her,' he admitted. 'I miss Marianne. All of you.'

For a moment, Elinor felt something approaching pity.

But Willoughby went on. 'And instead I am forced to pretend to love another woman. A cruel sort. You know she was the one who made me write to Marianne? Send back the hair?'

The pity dissipated. 'Again, you pass the blame to others. You deserve every second of your misery. It's your wife I feel sorry for.' And with that she dismissed him.

'I shall live in dread, then,' he said from the doorstep.

'Of what?' demanded Elinor, her patience long gone.

'Marianne's marriage. For then she will be truly lost to me.'

'Oh, Willoughby.' Elinor almost laughed at the audacity. 'Don't you see? She is lost to you already,' she said, and slammed the door firmly in his face.

CHAPTER FORTY

For a short while, Elinor stood motionless, her head crowded with thoughts – of Willoughby's nerve, his begging for forgiveness, his terrible fate to be stuck in a loveless marriage. But by the time the second set of wheels made their mark on the gravel, she found to her surprise that her heart was just as full – with relief at Marianne's recovery, with appreciation for Colonel Brandon's kindness, and with joy at her mother's arrival.

Their reunion was tearful. However, having been informed quickly of Marianne's rallying, these turned into tears of happiness, and Mrs Dashwood was soon at her middle daughter's bedside, telling her and Elinor tales of their sister Margaret's terrible French and apparent disinterest in reciting the Kings and Queens by heart. 'I'm sure she will do it for you, though,' she told Marianne. 'As soon as you're home.'

'Home,' repeated Marianne happily, closing her eyes at the thought, and falling rather swiftly into a peaceful sleep.

If Mrs Dashwood had been happy to see Marianne in spirits, she was happy too to let her slumber, for she had things she needed to discuss with Elinor as a matter of urgency.

'Colonel Brandon!' she announced, as soon as they were out of earshot. 'He's in love with Marianne! He told me so himself.'

'Really?' said Elinor, feigning surprise, as she hardly wanted to steal her mother's thunder.

'Oh, yes. He opened up to me in the carriage here. Quite besotted, he is. And so worried about her welfare. He would make the finest of husbands for either of you, really. The finest! But Marianne needs him more, given everything.'

'Of course,' said Elinor, not bothering to point out that she had never had feelings for the Colonel, nor he for her.

'And so much better than Willoughby,' added Mrs Dashwood. 'Worthless man that he is.'

Now that, Elinor could agree with wholeheartedly.

'Of course, I saw it all along. There was something about his eyes. Something wicked.'

'Quite,' agreed Elinor.

'The Colonel, though,' her mother went on. 'His eyes could not hide a thing. No, Marianne will be far happier with him than she would ever have been with Willoughby, even if he hadn't turned out to be a scoundrel.'

How perfectly it had all worked out, they agreed.

The only sticking point would be getting Marianne to see it.

CHAPTER FORTY-ONE

Within a week – a week in which a devoted Colonel Brandon barely left her side – Marianne was declared well enough to return to Barton.

'You must take my carriage,' insisted the Colonel. 'I can follow on by horse.'

'And visit soon?' checked Mrs Dashwood.

'Of course,' he replied. 'As soon as you're settled again, and Marianne completely better.' And, though Marianne's goodbye to him was no more than that of a good friend, he seemed to bloom with the same hope as her mother that this would soon grow to match his own affection.

★ ★ ★

Marianne's happiness certainly blossomed the moment she entered Barton Cottage. She took delight in every book, every piece of sheet music, even in her sister's recitation of the monarchs, which at least now proceeded past King John.

'I cannot wait to see the Park,' she declared. 'I must visit the library – I have missed reading so. Though the Colonel has offered to lend me several volumes.'

'I'm sure he has!' said Mrs Dashwood, delighted.

This mention, though, was as close as Marianne would get to declaring anything.

Worse, it was as clear as ever to Elinor that Willoughby was still on her sister's mind.

'Here is where it happened,' Marianne declared, as they walked up the hill behind the cottage the next morning. 'Right here, he lifted me, and I knew then my heart was his.'

'And . . . is it still?' asked Elinor tentatively.

Marianne paused. 'Do you know what?' she said. 'I don't feel anything. Not even regret, for I am done with that. My illness has allowed me to think. I realise my own behaviour hasn't been blameless. My hankering for passion blinded me to the man's faults. My desire for drama meant I indulged my own illness instead of trying to fight. If I had died, it would have been self-destruction. I only wish . . .'

'What?' urged Elinor. 'What do you wish?'

'I only wish I knew *why* Willoughby had behaved as he did.'

Elinor, remembering Willoughby's confession, steeled herself. 'If you knew, do you think it would make everything better?'

'Yes. I believe it would.'

And so Elinor told her sister everything – his visit when he thought Marianne might be dying, his debt, his desperation. She told her too that he still couldn't see that he was to blame, preferring to put it all down to circumstance.

Marianne paled at the tale, and tears were indeed shed. But at the end she held her sister's hand tight, and said simply, 'I see it now. I see what you see.'

Elinor squeezed her hand back. 'We can move on, then?' she asked.

'Yes,' said Marianne. 'We can move on.'

If only Elinor had remembered that she, too, had her ghost of Barton past. And he was surely due to come calling.

CHAPTER FORTY-TWO

It was more than a week later, the Dashwoods seated at a merry dinner at the cottage, when their servant, Tom, happened to announce that Mr Ferrars was married.

Marianne yelped.

Elinor, who had thought herself immune to such news, found herself wanting to do the same. Instead she said, 'Where did you hear that?'

'Exeter, ma'am. I seen him myself. And his lady – Miss Steele as was. She asked after you, asked to pass on her compliments.'

'Thank you,' said Elinor eventually. 'That's very kind.'

Marianne frowned. 'And it was definitely him? Definitely Mr Ferrars.'

'Saw him with my own eyes,' said Tom, slightly put out that his account was being doubted. 'They was in the carriage together. Quite the happy couple. Said they'd come and see you soon.'

'We shall look forward to it,' said Mrs Dashwood, trying to catch Elinor's eye.

Elinor smiled at her, but only in relief. Because she knew that it was an empty promise. There was no chance Edward would come, not after the last time. It had all been too awkward. Now, given the marriage, it would be even more so.

'Did he look well?' she asked at last.

'Very,' said Tom.

'Good,' said Elinor. And that was the last she would say on the matter, for that was *all* that mattered. Edward was Lucy's now, and glad to be so.

She must be happy for them and, moreover, put them out of her mind completely.

That, though, was easier said than done, and for days she found her fickle mind wandering to thoughts of Edward again: why had he married so quickly? He couldn't have taken orders yet. Though, she supposed, they would head to Delaford soon.

Delaford. How she had longed to go there. Still, perhaps if Marianne and Colonel Brandon— But, no, it would be too painful, surely? Seeing the pair of them in the parsonage together.

And where *was* Colonel Brandon, for that matter? Mrs Dashwood had written to him days ago, saying Marianne was fully restored and ready to receive visitors.

As if she might conjure him just by willpower, she leaned towards the window and scoured the gardens and out through the gate. And then she gasped.

For there, indeed, was a man, astride a gleaming horse, making his slow but determined way towards the cottage. But, unless she was imagining it, it was not Colonel Brandon.

But the bridegroom himself.

Mr Edward Ferrars.

CHAPTER FORTY-THREE

Elinor peered out the window at the figure again. No, it was not the Colonel. This man was decidedly Edward-like in shape and manner, as he dismounted precariously and walked cautiously up the path.

She sat down in surprise. 'I *will* be calm,' she told herself. 'I will *not* get upset.'

Marianne and Mrs Dashwood rushed in, the former pale, the latter red as a cherry.

'We saw from the upstairs window,' said Mrs Dashwood. 'Is it really him?'

Elinor could only nod, for it was very definitely Edward.

Not another syllable passed aloud, for they all waited in silence for Edward's entrance, hearing the knock on the door, the creak as it opened, the heavy steps that slapped on the flagstones. So it was to a room of closed mouths and frowns that Edward entered, his obvious agitation only increasing.

It was Mrs Dashwood who spoke first. 'We're all very pleased for you,' she said.

'I– I–,' stammered a red-faced Edward in reply.

Elinor wished she could match her mother's congratulations, but the words seemed stuck in her throat. Marianne, too, was dumbstruck. Even Margaret seemed clear that she should maintain a dignified silence and sat quietly in the corner.

But this was impossible. Someone had to say something. *Elinor* had to say something. 'Pleasant weather we're having,' she blurted at last. Then scolded herself silently for thinking up such trivia.

'Is . . . Mrs Ferrars well?' asked Mrs Dashwood, after Edward had agreed the weather was, indeed, pleasant.

'Quite well,' said Edward.

'And she's in Exeter?' checked Elinor, hoping Lucy wouldn't pop up at any moment.

Edward frowned. 'No,' he replied, apparently perplexed. 'My mother is in town.'

'Oh, I meant Mrs Edward Ferrars,' said Elinor, with some difficulty. She dared not look up. She could hardly bear that he was here at all, that she was going through this hideous business.

Edward frowned. 'Perhaps you mean Mrs Robert Ferrars? That is to say, my brother's wife?'

'Your brother's wife?' repeated Marianne and Mrs Dashwood in unison.

Elinor met Edward's eyes finally. 'I don't understand,' she said.

'You do not know? No, you must not,' blustered Edward, fiddling inexplicably with his cuffs. 'I see it now. It's just that my brother . . . is lately married. To . . . to Miss Steele.'

Marianne's eyes were practically on stalks. 'He married Nancy?' she demanded, asking what everyone was thinking.

'Oh, no, not her, not Nancy,' Edward managed. Then he stared at Elinor as if willing something between them. 'Lucy.'

Mrs Dashwood gasped.

'Lucy?' whispered Elinor, hardly daring to believe it.

'Yes. He married Lucy. And so I wondered . . . That is . . . if you still . . . if you'd like . . .'

'What?' demanded Marianne. 'Spit it out!'

Edward met Elinor's gaze. 'I wondered, now I am free, if *you* might marry *me*.'

CHAPTER FORTY-FOUR

But how could Elinor even consider Edward's proposal? you might think (Marianne certainly did). *He led her on and all the while been engaged to another!*

But he hadn't, not in Elinor's head. He had simply met her at a time when he was no longer available. And though he had grand feelings for her, as she had him, he had put those aside in order to keep the promise he had already made. And rightly so. But, put on the spot, Lucy had found that 'making do' on a vicar's wage was less tolerable than she had previously thought, and therefore decided she preferred the considerably

richer Robert after all. So she had released
Edward from his promise, and he could confess
the truth at last: he loved Elinor. Adored her, no
less.

And she him.

And so she said yes, and, not a month later,
dressed in delicate white lace, she
said 'I do'.

It was this that helped
Marianne realise that a
man might, indeed,
be capable of more
than one great love.
For, as her sister had
discovered her own
romantic sensibilities,
Marianne had, at last,
become exceptionally
sensible. And so, it

was not too much of a surprise that, six months later, she echoed her sister's vows and finally wed the man who had never once shown her anything but devotion.

Mrs Marianne Brandon now lives happily at Delaford, no more than a mile from her sister. Mrs Dashwood and Margaret visit their happy homes often, but are content still in Barton Cottage, humble though it may be.

And what of Fanny? And the dreaded Mrs Ferrars?

Well, the latter was so outraged to be betrayed by not one but two sons, she took to her bed. Distraught, Fanny made John write to Elinor begging for a letter from Edward, and a regretful one at that. Edward must tell their mother how sorry he was. How wrong he was to go against her wishes. How much he was suffering. Then, kind-hearted as she was, their mother would surely forgive him.

But Edward told his new wife he was neither sorry, nor believed he was wrong. And instead of suffering, he was the happiest he had been in his life.

And as they walked hand-in-hand in the bluebell woods before dinner, Elinor thought of the home she had grown up in, Norland, and realised that, far from longing for its splendour, she was glad to be at Delaford with Edward.

The parsonage may be small, and she may not be wealthy, but her life, like that of her sister, had never been richer.

A NOTE FROM JOANNA

Firstly, a confession: until I came to be offered the opportunity to rewrite *Sense and Sensibility*, the closest I had come to Jane Austen was TV re-runs of Mr Darcy emerging wet from a lake, and a reluctant trudge around her house with an obsessive friend. Not even my grandmother's entreaties to the thirteen-year-old-bookworm me that 'it's feminist, it's funny' could persuade me away from my pony novels and into the pages populated by the Bennets, the Elliots, the Dashwoods. 'Too old-fashioned,' I am sure I whined. *Too uncool*, I am sure I thought.

Well, it may have taken more than three decades, but I quickly realised the folly of my own pride and prejudice, and have now eaten my ill-chosen words, for Austen is modern and relevant, as well as being funny and, yes, feminist. Though the world she paints is markedly different to our own, the heroines of *Sense and Sensibility*, Marianne and Elinor, are recognisable and endearing. We root for them in their endurance of the customs of the time, and in their pursuit by various men; we boo as Willoughby snubs the impassioned Marianne, and cheer as patient Elinor gets her Edward. There is something to learn here, about the predicament of women in the late Regency period, but more importantly, much to love. I hope you fall as hard for Jane Austen as I have done. Because there are many more treasures to read after this one.

A NOTE FROM ÉGLANTINE

My name is Églantine Ceulemans, and as you might have noticed thanks to my first name . . . I am French!

In France, we tend to associate Britain with wonderful English gardens, a unique sense of humour, William Shakespeare and, last but not least, Jane Austen!

It was such an honour to have the opportunity

to illustrate Jane Austen's stories. I have always enjoyed reading books that are filled with love, laughter and happy endings, and Austen writes all of those things brilliantly. And who wouldn't love to illustrate gorgeous dresses, stunning mansions and passionate young women standing up for their deep convictions? I also tried to do justice to Austen's humour and light-heartedness by drawing characterful people and adding in friendly pets (sometimes well-hidden and always witnessing intense but mostly funny situations!).

I discovered Jane Austen's work with *Pride and Prejudice* one sun-filled summer, and I have such good memories of sitting reading it in the garden beneath my grandmother's weeping willow. This setting definitely helped me to fall in love with the book, but it would be a lie to say that I wasn't moved by Elizabeth and Mr Darcy's love story and that I didn't laugh when her mother tried (with no shame at all) to marry her daughters to all the best catches in the town! I imagined all those characters in my head so vividly, and it was a real pleasure to finally illustrate them, alongside all Austen's other amazing characters.

Jane Austen is an author who managed to depict nineteenth-century England with surprising modernity. She questioned the morality of so-called well-to-do people and she managed to write smartly, sharply and independently, at a time where women were considered to be nothing if not married to a man. I hope that these illustrated versions of her books will help you to question the past and the present, without ever forgetting to laugh ... and to dream!

SO, WHO WAS JANE AUSTEN?

Jane Austen was born in 1775 and had seven siblings. Her parents were well-respected in their local community, and her father was the clergyman for a nearby parish. She spent much of her life helping to run the family home, whilst reading and writing in her spare time.

✳ JANE AUSTEN ✳

Jane began to anonymously publish her work in her thirties and four of her novels were released during her lifetime: *Sense and Sensibility*, *Pride and Prejudice*, *Mansfield Park* and *Emma*. However, at the age of forty-one she became ill, eventually dying in 1817. Her two remaining novels, *Northanger Abbey* and *Persuasion*, were published after her death.

Austen's books are well-known for their comedy, wit and irony. Her observations about wealthy society, and especially the role women played in it, were unlike anything that had been published before. Her novels were not widely read or praised until years later, but they have gone on to leave a mark on the world for ever, inspiring countless poems, books, plays and films.

AND WHAT WAS IT LIKE IN 1811?

HOW DID INHERITANCE WORK?

During the Regency era, the law in England ruled that property (which included buildings, belongings and money) was to be inherited by the closest male heir to the owner – often this was the firstborn son, but it could also be a cousin. This explains why when Henry Dashwood dies, Norland estate is automatically inherited by John Dashwood, even though Henry also leaves behind a widow and three daughters – Mrs Dashwood, Elinor, Marianne and Margaret.

This inheritance law was designed to prevent property from being divided between multiple relatives. To modern readers this law can seem very unfair because it meant that younger sons often inherited very little, and daughters such as Marianne and Elinor might find themselves dependent on others to take care of them.

COULD PEOPLE BE DISINHERITED?

In some cases, heirs were **disinherited** – this meant that they did not have any property passed on to them, even though they were the lawful heir. This usually only happened if they were seen to have brought shame upon their family. In *Sense and Sensibility*, Mrs Ferrars disinherits Edward when she finds out that he is engaged to Lucy Steele. The reason for this disinheritance is because of Lucy's social standing – she does not come from a particularly wealthy family and therefore wouldn't be able to advance Edward's position in society, something that Mrs Ferrars can't abide. As a result, the Ferrars' inheritance passes down to Robert, Edward's younger brother.

WAS IT COMMON FOR PEOPLE TO HAVE SECOND HOMES?

Only the well-off could afford two homes – often this meant a townhouse in London or Bath, and a large manor house in the countryside. Much of the population lived in small, overcrowded houses. Characters like John Dashwood and Mrs Jennings both have second homes in London that they visit regularly so they can socialise, attend the theatre and enjoy balls, whilst the Palmers have a country estate in Cleveland.

WHAT WAS A POORHOUSE?

A poorhouse, otherwise known as a workhouse, was a place that provided food and shelter in return for hard and often unpleasant work. Poorhouses took in people who were sick, elderly, abandoned or orphaned – it was a last resort for those that could no longer support themselves. Colonel Brandon explains to Elinor that after his brother divorces his wife, she is forced to live and work in a poorhouse. He finds her thin, pale and coughing blood, which was mostly likely the result of the awful conditions she would have suffered.

COLLECT THEM ALL!

JANE AUSTEN'S
PERSUASION

WITTY WORDS BY **NARINDER DHAMI**
DELIGHTFUL DOODLES BY **ÉGLANTINE CEULEMANS**

JANE AUSTEN'S
MANSFIELD PARK

WITTY WORDS BY **AYISHA MALIK**
DELIGHTFUL DOODLES BY **ÉGLANTINE CEULEMANS**

JANE AUSTEN'S
NORTHANGER ABBEY

WITTY WORDS BY **STEVEN BUTLER**
DELIGHTFUL DOODLES BY **ÉGLANTINE CEULEMANS**